Praise for From the Crooked Timber

"Okla Elliott's new story collection has a terrific variety of characters—all of them credible, sympathetic, and complex, presented in Elliott's lean, compelling, breezy style. Elliott has a sharp perception of character and a balanced wisdom about how his characters think and feel. He is a fine craftsman, and each story here is a pleasure to read and to contemplate."

> —Thomas E. Kennedy, best-selling author of *In the Company of Angels*

"In the gritty, tough-minded, open-hearted stories of *From the Crooked Timber*, Okla Elliott explores lives of quiet desperation, and sometimes stolen consolations, beneath the crush of instant-access, celebrity-culture media. With broken families and fractured relationships of the kinds Elliott lays bare ever more the rule than the exception, an imagination such as his is one the culture would do well to hear."

> —Jonathan Monroe, author of *Demosthenes' Legacy* and Professor of Comparative Literature at Cornell University

"The seeming ease and clarity of the prose—the hardest thing to achieve in writing of any kind—makes many appearances."

> —Franz Wright, Pulitzer Prize-winning author of *Kindertotenwald*

"Elliott's forceful and unpredictable stories speak compellingly of love thwarted, connections not pursued, or severed quickly before they can deepen. Elliott's honesty and his insight into human desires, the passions that hold humans hostage, life tumbling from one experience to another, are darkly luminous. Bleakly beautiful."

> —Duff Brenna, author of *Too Cool* (a *New York Times* Notable Book)

"Okla Elliott's work will thrill you. His characters are as real as your own family . . . Elliott writes as if death and loss can be comic, and in his hands, they are—ruefully comic."

> —Kelly Cherry, three-time winner of the PEN/Syndicated Fiction Award

FROM THE CROOKED TIMBER

From the Crooked Timber

a novella & stories

OKLA ELLIOTT

Press 53
Winston-Salem

Press 53, LLC
PO Box 30314
Winston-Salem, NC 27130

First Edition

Copyright © 2011 by Okla Elliott

Cover design by Kevin Morgan Watson

Cover art, "Bullet Hole" Copyright © 2011 by Ivana Krušec

Author photo by Robert B. MacCready

Library of Congress Control Number: 2011919756

Printed on acid-free paper
ISBN 978-1-935708-47-6

From the crooked timber of humanity,
no straight thing can ever be made.

—Immanuel Kant

Acknowledgments

The author would like to thank the editors of the following journals and anthologies where several of the stories in this collection originally appeared.

"The Queen of Limbo" appeared in *Another Chicago Magazine* and the *Press 53 Spotlight Anthology 2011*.

"The Long Walk Home" appeared in the *Press 53 Spotlight Anthology 2011*.

"The Good Earth, the Mud" appeared in *Muse* (published by the Cleveland Arts Council).

"Lonely Tylenol" appeared in *Contemporary World Literature* and the *Press 53 Spotlight Anthology 2011*.

"The Kidnapping" appeared in *Monkeybicycle* (Dzanc Books).

Contents

The Queen of Limbo

When I first saw Sylvie, she was standing on the island of an eight-lane road, no place for a girl of ten maybe twelve to be standing. She was wearing a blue sundress. Cornflower blue, like the crayon from when I was a kid. Traffic flow was heavy, so I had to cross a few lanes and missed the chance to pull a u-turn. I ended up whipping around in a Hardee's parking lot and getting back on the road. I was worried she'd be gone, or worse, in the time it took. But there she stood, blue sundress on a concrete island. I pulled up beside her and put on my hazard lights. Keri, my ex, would have told me I was crazy to do such a thing.

"You okay? Did you get lost?" She looked at me like I was the weirdest thing she'd ever seen. "Are you scared? Trying to get home?" Still no response. "Why don't you let me give you a ride?"

"I'm not s'posed to talk to strangers. Mom tells me that."

"You shouldn't. Your mom's right. But not this time," I said.

She looked me over, considering.

"I'm a school teacher," I lied. "I'll give you a lift home."

By this time, cars were waiting behind me, drivers looking over their shoulders to switch lanes, then turning back to lay on their horns. I know how it must have looked to the other drivers, but I didn't give a damn about them. Sylvie looked at the cars. She looked at my face. I reached back and unlocked the door just behind me, so she wouldn't have to walk around the car in traffic. She glanced at the honking cars and jumped in fast and slammed the door.

I started driving but left my hazards on until I got up enough speed to be part of the normal flow of traffic. In the drink holder, a waxed fast food cup had little beads of condensation streaking down its slick surface. I took a gulp of Sunkist and Aristocrat gin through the straw and nearly gagged on the waxy flavor the drink had absorbed from the cup. In the rearview mirror I could see the girl squirming, trying to latch her seatbelt.

"Where do you live?"

"I'm not going there," she announced, as though talking to a dimwitted younger brother. "I'm going to the Pink's Skate Rink. Tonight's the limbo contest and whoever wins gets to skate for free all night." Then, awed at the prospect, "Even the late skate is free for who wins the limbo contest."

She fidgeted with the latch of the seatbelt.

"It's broken," I said.

The girl tossed the seatbelt away from her and climbed into the front passenger seat. Her sundress rubbed against my face as she passed by. Once settled, she clicked her seatbelt into place. I took in her satisfied look and felt calmer for it.

"You know where the rink is?"

"Yeah. It's only a couple of miles. A long way to walk though."

"Not so long," she said and turned to look out the window. "My name's Sylvie."

"Mine's Jasper."

"My real name's Sylvia, but I like Sylvie better. My mom hates it," she said. "Now we're not strangers anymore."

"Are you hungry, Sylvie? I saw a Hardee's back there a bit." I drank more of my Sunkist and gin. No urge to gag this time.

In the Hardee's drive-thru, I bought us spicy chicken sandwiches and french fries. Sylvie ate noisily beside me as I drove. We threw the wrappers away in the trash can in front of Pink's Skate Rink. Sylvie marched straight to the counter and blurted out her skate size. She'd already slipped her shoes off, stepping on each heel with her last two steps to the counter.

"I need a five dollar deposit," a woman with nicotine-stained fingers and dyed-red hair said.

"But I don't have five dollars."

"You got to have money for a deposit, and skating ain't free."

"I don't need money. I'm going to win the limbo contest."

"I'm sure you will, honey," the woman said as she lit a cigarette.

Keri would be at home surfing the internet, searching for Soviet-era army medals or propaganda posters. That's all she really ever did anymore—look for more of her Soviet stuff on the internet—except when she was teaching intro to Russian at the university. You could say she was obsessed. She told me once that a woman in the Ukraine was selling her placenta for a thousand American dollars over the internet. "What sort of international mailing restrictions does that violate?" I joked, but she didn't laugh, just kept clicking thumbnails of Siberian art and pocket watches engraved with the cityscape of Moscow.

"I'll pay the deposit." I peeled a five free from the money clip Keri had given me last Christmas, a nice metal job with engraved Cyrillic letters, another one of her internet finds. Sylvie sat in a hard plastic seat and laced her skates.

"I've got to get warmed up."

She skated round the rink and I went to the snack bar to order a fresh Sunkist. I figured I could slip out to the car for a minute and load it up with gin.

"Don't have Sunkist, man. Is Slice okay?"

"Same thing. Give me a large."

On the way to the car, I saw a cigarette machine, and though I'd quit smoking back when Keri was pregnant for a few months, I fed the four dollars in and got a pack of Camel filters. In the parking lot, my legs hanging out of the opened car door, I squeezed the plastic half-gallon jug of gin and hotboxed a Camel. I remembered Keri, the way she'd moped around the house for weeks, and me not knowing what to say or do. My drink tasted different, and I thought maybe Sunkist and Slice aren't the same after all until I remembered that this was a fresh cup and there hadn't been time yet for the waxy flavor to seep in.

Back inside the rink I sat in an uncomfortable seat and drank. I was getting drunk. The skin on the back of my hands was warm, and the swoosh of skaters going by and that rattle-whir from the ball bearings in the wheels made me lightheaded. I couldn't think straight. I wondered if I should call Keri, tell her what I was doing. She'd get kick out of a skate rink. She'd changed her number again, but through the coming gin fog I could remember most of it. It had fives, nines, and zeros. I'd gotten it from her friend Leigh. I told her that Keri still had my DVDs and I needed to get in touch with her to get them back.

"Ain't you gonna skate, Jasper?" Sylvie was beside me. I hadn't roller-skated since I was fourteen.

"You know what? I just remembered. I won the limbo contest the last time I was in a roller rink."

"You won't win this time." She sized up her competition. "You're too big."

"Oh, I'm not even going to try. I just remembered. That's all." I didn't mention I might vomit orange if I bent over to go under the limbo stick.

I tied the skates too tight but didn't bother to fix them. Sylvie grabbed my hand and set our pace. The weightless glide around the rink cleared my head, and I knew nothing good could come of me calling Keri. It was just that every time I saw or did something I thought she might enjoy, I wanted to call her and share it. Like telling her made it better, or that if it was good enough what I told her, she'd love me more for it.

"What do you teach?"

"Huh?"

"I said, What do you teach?"

"Oh, that. Math. Middle school. Algebra mostly." It was a

reasonable lie. I was working as an actuary at the time. (*Actually, I'm an actuary*, shot through my head, and I wanted to laugh at how funny it sounded.)

"I hate math."

"Me too," I said.

Back in line at the snack bar I asked for a refill, but the cashier told me there were no free refills, so I paid full price. I unlaced my skates and went to the car in sock feet. The asphalt's warmth was relaxing, a sort of heat massage for my feet. I gave the gin bottle a couple of hearty squeezes and lit a Camel. I stood beside the car, letting my feet absorb the asphalt's warmth. I hadn't felt anything so soothing in a long time. I lay down on my back and dragged on my Camel and watched as I puffed the stars in and out of existence. I found the Big Dipper, or Ursa Major as the astronomy textbooks would have it. Who in hell saw those seven stars and thought of a big bear? I wiggled my toes and knew I'd better get back inside. The limbo contest was about to start, and I wanted to watch Sylvie win it. I'd scoped out the other kids and no one looked like they were better on skates than she was. And no one wanted it as badly.

Two employees—a fat teenage girl and an athletic woman of maybe thirty—held the limbo stick on either end as the kids lined up. The first go everyone made it with room to spare. Then the fat girl and the athletic woman lowered it a few inches. All but one made it that time. And so forth. It came down to Sylvie and a young boy with disheveled clothes and hair, like he hadn't had a bath for a while and was accustomed to it. Sylvie made it under again, and the limbo stick was lowered. The cashier at the snack bar watched, chewing on a Snickers. The dirty boy went under, but on his way up lost his balance and fell with a bony thud. He kicked the floor with his heels and began to cry. Sylvie skated straight to me and threw her arms around my waist, screeching her joy into my chest. I put my hands on her back and felt her ribs through the cornflower blue sundress. The fabric was nice to rub and I felt each rib and the soft space between each rib as my hands rubbed up and down her back.

The athletic woman was helping the crying boy get up. He jerked free from her and began skating around the rink, picking up as much speed as he could manage. He just kept pumping his legs, picking up speed, going in circles. Sylvie was dubbed The Queen of Limbo over the loudspeaker. There was much cheering and flashing of lights.

"My mom picks me up when she gets off work." Sylvie was worrying a loose thread in the hem of her dress between her thumb and forefinger. "I won't get to stay for the late skate, but maybe I can tell the lady that I want you to be able to skate it in my place. I might not've made it on time, if you hadn't given me a ride here." People were crowding back into the rink, and Sylvie went in with them. I looked at my feet and saw I was still in sock feet and decided I should go out and have another cigarette and drink to celebrate Sylvie's win.

Soon as I crossed the threshold of Pink's Skate Rink and felt the humid summer air on my arms and face, I pulled out my cell phone and dialed. 5-0-8-4-0...; her number came flooding back to me. It went straight to voice mail, as I had expected. Keri had rarely answered her phone in all the years I knew her. She would go through phases where she would answer "just to prove I'm not crazy," though I never saw why answering a phone or not answering it was such a big deal. Me, I always answer.

Hello, this is Keri. Leave a message. That voice. I hung up without leaving a message but found her number in my call history and hit the little green button again. *Hello, this is Keri. Leave a message.* "Hey, I know I probably shouldn't be calling. Definitely shouldn't be, I mean, but I wanted to tell you about this little girl I met, named Sylvie, Sylvia really, but Sylvie is much better, don't you think? Anyway, she just won the limbo contest down here at Pink's Skate Rink. Bet you'd never think to see me at a skate rink. But, anyway, call me. We could get a beer and talk. I'd really like that, and..." I was cut off by that beep which meant she hadn't erased any messages for a month or more and there was no space left for me.

Back inside, the rink was thick with skaters, and I couldn't find Sylvie at first. Then I saw her with the dirty boy who'd come in second. They'd suspended the limbo stick on the backs of two chairs and were practicing. Sylvie took sips from his Coke like it was hers. The boy had a skittish way about him that made me sad, but it looked like Sylvie's attentions were cheering him up. In front of me in line, a boy ordered a suicide in a thick drawl. He was acting tough like a movie saloon cowboy. "Give me another suicide, light on the ice," he said, and looked over his shoulder at a group of older kids who stared at him menacingly. I sat there sucking down my own drink and watching Sylvie, thinking how if things had gone different with Keri, we could have had a daughter named Sylvie. She was such a beautiful little girl, the way only smart girls in cornflower blue sundresses can be.

Sylvie rolled over to me and said her mom would be there soon and that she was supposed to wait outside for her. She returned her skates and collected her pass for the late skate. "Can I give it to Jasper to skate?" she asked the smoking woman.

"Sweetie, you can do anything you want to. You're The Queen of Limbo," she said and laughed.

Sylvie handed me the pass and we went outside. I don't know what I was thinking. I guess I figured I could just walk away when her mother showed up. Just before we got to the door, I lifted her up and sat her on my shoulder. "All make way for The Queen of Limbo," I said, and Sylvie giggled as I kicked the door open with great flourish and walked us into the parking lot. Her skinny legs batted against my chest and the rustle of her dress was in my right ear louder than the rest of the world. The weight of her on my shoulder was pleasant.

"Look up there." I pointed out the Big Dipper. "That's not its real name. Ursa Major, which means 'big bear' in Greek or maybe Latin, is its real name."

Sylvie began squirming, trying to get down off my shoulder. A woman dressed in turquoise scrubs was walking toward us. The skin under her eyes was a reddish gray I'd seen in my face the day after a long drunk, or when I'd stay up all night working at the computer. I would probably look like that tomorrow morning. The only thing animating her face was surprise and something else I couldn't place.

"What the hell is going on here? Sylvia, who is this man?" I sat Sylvie down, and her mother motioned her away from me and under her protective arm. The loose fabric of her shirt half-covered Sylvie's face, a sight I'll never forget.

"Who are you?" she asked.

"I picked her up. She was stranded on the island and I thought that was unsafe."

"Stranded on an island?" she said. "Sylvia, did he hurt you?"

"I was worried she'd get run over," I said, trying to get the conversation under control. I almost ran to my car and drove off. Then I thought to step closer and try to explain, but I was worried she might smell the gin on my breath, so I backed away, holding my hands palm up, showing her I held no violence in them.

"Hey, mom, did you know that the Big Dipper isn't its real name?" Sylvie asked.

"Shut up, Sylvia," she said. "Now, tell me who you are or I'm calling the cops."

"God, Mom, he's my math teacher, Mr. Powell," she said. "You talked to him last month on the phone about my stupid C-minus in pre-algebra."

A spark of recognition came across the woman's face. She really had talked to a Mr. Powell about Sylvie's grade, I thought. I was proud of Sylvie. The ability to tell a good lie is the sign of true intelligence. I should know; I was married to a woman who graduated *cum laude* from Duke. Keri used to say how our kid was going to be some kind of genius, and I never doubted it. Sylvie's mother looked at me, and I smiled, trying to hide my surprise—and trying to look like a math teacher. I smiled the nervous smile I figured a math teacher would have. I shrugged my shoulders, but I still didn't say anything. My hands were sweaty, and I was worried I'd slur, though Keri used to tell me I didn't slur, no matter how drunk I got. "Maybe boozing is my calling in life," I told her, grinning a big dopey grin. "I'm just so damned good at it."

The woman looked at Sylvie's face. I figured Sylvie was a handful, always getting into trouble and always finding a slick way out. And that's when it hit me that I'd probably never see Sylvie again. Her mother would take her home and their lives would continue and so would mine. It wasn't even that I wanted to see her again. It just seemed sad that I wouldn't.

"Yeah, I saw Sylvia walking to the roller rink and recognized her from class, so I stopped and gave her a lift," I said. "And then I thought I should stay around until you got here."

Sylvie looked up at me, smiling.

"I guess I'll be seeing you on Monday, Sylvia," I said.

"I'm . . . sorry," her mother said, and I felt bad for her. It seemed wrong that she should feel embarrassed.

"You have a wonderful daughter," I said. "It's obvious how much she's loved. I wish all my students were as fortunate as Sylvia."

"Thank you, Mr. Powell," her mother said.

I watched them drive off. I stood there as the little sedan shrank into the distance and finally took a left turn out of my view. There were voices behind me in the parking lot, a man and a woman arguing on their way out of the roller rink.

The pass for the late skate was still in my hand. On the way back in I threw what was left of the Camels in the trash. The rink was dull with Sylvie gone. The boy who ordered suicides like a cowboy sat with a pretty, redheaded girl, their hands underneath the table. One of the older kids who were staring at him earlier was fuming. The dirty boy was skating backwards and doing a good job of it. I tapped the pass for the late skate against the palm of my hand and sat down to tie my skates back on.

I floated drunk, the whir and clack of the skates' wheels rolling the world beneath me, and I didn't let myself call Keri. I wanted to talk to her so bad the weight of the cell phone in my pocket made my leg tingle, but I knew I would never speak to her again. It had all happened, and there was no reversing it with words. But if things had been different, I would have called her and talked in a voice so stripped down and bare no one could refuse it. "I'm in no condition to drive, baby," I'd say. "Come down here and get me out of this place."

They Live on the Water

Denis's brothers have gained weight, fifteen maybe twenty pounds since last he's seen them. This is due to both of them being failures, being poor, he thinks. Poor people eat at McDonald's, eat bacon and sausage, drink whole milk for breakfast. And when he hugged them earlier, both smelled of cigarette smoke. Poor people smoke. Don't go to the gym. He tensed his flat stomach when their soft bellies pressed against him, turned his head away from their cigarette breath. But how could he be thinking about this, with his wife crying beside him, and his ten-year-old daughter being lowered slowly in her coffin, cradled in chains, by some mechanized contraption he doesn't want to know the name for? Fucking insane.

They decided to bury Jane back home, where they had grown up and met and been engaged. Elena still drives here to visit her mother every weekend, occasionally stopping by to see Denis's mother as well. *It's only an hour away, Denis. No biggie, alright?* She picked that one up from Jane. *Can I go to the dance, Daddy? Can I stay over at Lucy's? It's no biggie, Daddy, really.* He doesn't even want to think the goddamned words. But he never makes a fuss, not one to speak of anyway, about Elena's trips. And when she says that *someone* has to keep in touch with their families, he lets that go by, doesn't take her bait for an argument, though he doesn't understand why she wants to go back. When he left Hickory, North Carolina, it was for good. But the last few months, since the incident (or, The Incident as he's begun thinking of it spitefully, because no one wants to talk about what happened), Elena has been going every couple of days, leaving him alone in the house with his thoughts and with Jane's ghostly room.

The expensive coffin thuds when it touches earth. Elena cries more loudly when she hears it thud. There's a grinding of gears as the contraption somehow retracts the straps and chains. Someone invented that thing, Denis thinks, and is to this day earning dividends on its continued use. Denis wishes he'd bought the more expensive coffin now. He'd spent over four thousand, but he should have spent more. At the time, it seemed ridiculous to worry about what he buried Jane in. Now, he feels like he skimped, like he told his dead daughter she wasn't worth an extra grand or two. He closes his eyes and tries to stop thinking.

The preacher talks about God and circles of life and a bunch of other shit Denis can't listen to. He looks into the barren, calligraphic trees, and wants to find some comfort or meaning in their bare branches. Calligraphic. He'd read that description of trees in a book he'd liked, but he can't remember which book right now, just that he'd liked it. He looks at his shiny shoes and thinks how stupid shiny shoes are. The grass beneath his feet. The curve of his wife's waist, the black leggings she's wearing, a freckle on her neck. Sex enters his mind. He thinks how Jane grew inside Elena. They haven't had sex since Jane disappeared. He wants to have sex. Stop thinking, just stop. Please, let me stop. Eyes closed, he lets his head fall back. He is surprised to feel tears on his neck.

Jimmy, his oldest brother, goes into a coughing fit, phlegm cracking in his chest. Denis watches him look around for a place to spit. Hard to find a place to spit at a funeral, isn't it, asshole? Denis closes his eyes again. It's not like I don't deserve all of this.

2

Watching it unfold on TV might have been the worst part. These fuckers are getting better ratings because of all this, he thought. Elena giving an interview, breaking down on local news. Photos of Jane. Jane in a swimming pool, its blue water glistening chlorine-clean behind her. Jane from the school yearbook. A casual photo of Jane reading on the living room floor. Denis squeezed his hands down on the armchair, trying to keep himself from smashing the television every time some new anchorman called it an ongoing tragedy, a mystery unsolved, a horror for everyone in Charlotte, North Carolina.

The police had assumed it was a kidnapping. There had been several in the area over the past year, a fat policeman, Officer Jenkins, told Denis and Elena. You might've seen something about them on the TV, he'd said, and Denis did remember something about a girl, age eleven or twelve, just about Jane's age, who had been found stabbed to death in a dumpster over in Davidson, down the road a bit. What a bastard, Denis thought. *That* is the last thing you want to tell us. He looked at his wife, but he could see that she didn't remember anything about other kidnappings, so he just nodded at the fat policeman and didn't say anything.

"Or she might be off horsing around with some friends. That happens too, you know," Officer Jenkins said to Elena. "That might be all it is."

But Denis could tell from the officer's voice that he didn't think that was all it was. They'd called all of Jane's friends, and none of them had seen her since the previous morning, and she wasn't answering the cell phone Elena made her carry when she was away from the house.

That night, exhausted from driving around the neighboring suburbs all day looking for Jane, they cooked dinner as usual but ate standing in the kitchen. He cut onions and tomatoes, and they both drank wine by the glassful. Elena propped herself against the sink and forked small pieces of pasta into her mouth while Denis leaned over the tile-topped island in the middle of the kitchen and smeared sauce around his plate with a piece of toast. Afterwards, they set the dishes in the sink and ran hot water over them, didn't bother to wash them.

"At least she's wearing her good wool coat," Elena said. It seemed like the first thing she'd said since Officer Jenkins had left hours ago. But that couldn't be right. She must have said something else.

"She's going to be okay," Denis said, staring at the greasy-red water in the sink. "I don't care what that fat fuck says." Denis stood there expecting her to act offended, to say something about his cursing. "Officer Fatkins," he said a few seconds later and barked a sharp burst of laughter.

"My god, Denis," Elena said and walked into the living room and sank on the couch. She watched the news reports for a while.

Denis poured himself another large glass of wine and drank it, wondering why he'd wanted to offend her at a time like this. He'd read some article about couples lashing out at each other during times of stress. Almost as if one of the duties of love was to be each other's punching bags. What a stupid way to be. He stared at the water in the sink—the yellowish, coagulating grease and the translucent red from the marinara. He wanted to clean the dishes but couldn't bear to put his hands in the water.

Now Elena was watching a movie from their collection— *The English Patient* or *The End of the Affair* or *Sophie's Choice*, some snooty smart shit like that; he couldn't tell which and didn't care to go into the living room to find out. He didn't know how long he'd been standing in the kitchen, looking at the water and drinking his wine. He walked down the hallway and climbed the stairs to his office where he would shuffle papers or maybe get some work done, though he doubted it. Just going through the motions, Denis would tell his partners in the coming weeks when they asked how he was doing.

On his office desk there was a photo of the three of them. Jane was just an infant then. She had been born three months premature and there was some question as to whether they would lose her. Denis remembered standing outside her little plastic cage, tubes taped to her body, machines all around. Her skin was so red and thin, so not-human. Larval. He had hated himself for thinking of his baby girl as anything but perfect, especially with Elena laid up in a bed two floors above in the hospital, recovering from the caesarian section. What kind of father am I?

As Jane grew into a little girl, Denis remembered his early impressions and doted on her, atoning for a sin no one else knew he'd committed. He would think about her all day at the office, and on his way home he'd stop by the toy store and buy whatever thing she'd been prattling about the previous night at the dinner table. Sometimes he'd just walk into the store and ask a worker what was popular these days, what did they sell the most of, and he would buy that, whatever it was and whatever the price. Sometimes he'd lie in the dark before going to sleep and think how close they'd come to losing her and what a bastard he was.

"I'm going back out to look for her," Elena said. He looked up from his desk and saw her backlit in the doorway of his office. "You want to come with me?"

He drove and she leaned out the window with a flashlight, yelling Jane's name occasionally. We must look like lunatics, Denis thought, but they kept at it until five a.m.

3

Denis looks over the grave and past the preacher, who is still talking, something about the bright light of God's love and the darkness of somethingsomething. Denis looks at Shari and Carl, who are standing toward the back, near the gate. He hasn't seen Shari for two years or more. She made Carl come, Denis thinks, and he wants to thank her, knowing how hard it must be on them to be here. Shari looks up and their eyes meet briefly before she turns her head to focus on the preacher. Denis notices that Carl is staring at him and looks at the ground.

4

Denis first met Carl through one of his clients. Carl owned a software development and troubleshooting company that was merging with another company specializing in hardware installation and repair. "We'll be a one-stop computer solution," Carl said and grinned at how smart he thought that sounded. Denis almost suggested that he make that the company motto but then realized it probably already was. Carl needed the merger done smoothly and quickly. The task would be simple enough, a few stock-phrased contracts with some slight rewording. He'd need to check the outstanding invoices for each company and make sure there were no breeches in either's Articles of Organization. But all in all, it was an easy job and so Denis agreed to take it, only padding the estimated billable hours by five, not his usual ten.

After it was all done, Carl had insisted on taking him out for dinner and drinks. He was from Texas, he told Denis, and Texans show their gratitude right.

"And my wife, Shari, and I have been wanting to get out on the town a bit more, meet some people," Carl said.

Denis was about to decline the offer but thought there might be more business to be had with Carl. "Why don't we go out on my boat?" Denis said. "There's a great restaurant on the lake where we can dock and go in to eat or have the food delivered to the boat."

"Excellent. Just fantastic."

5

When Denis and Elena had moved into the house on Lake Norman, Elena began keeping these little pastel post-it notes around the house. She had ones with bunnies, rainbows, fluffy clouds. He used to pick on her about them. "Ah, wook at the wittle bunnwies," he teased. He drew devil horns on a bunny or altered a leprechaun so that it was holding a huge, erect penis at the end of a rainbow. Elena rolled her eyes.

They'd gotten married the summer after graduation, before he matriculated at Carolina Law School and she began her MA in Spanish. Through those three years, they were careful that Elena didn't get pregnant. The last thing they needed was a financial burden like that. Popping out babies is how people back home kept themselves stuck in Hicksville. They knew at least half a dozen girls who had dropped out of school when they got pregnant. Denis's best friend in high school, Trace Reams, already had two kids from different mothers and was living with a third woman, the last Denis had heard.

But they wanted children. And so, after they'd moved in, Elena began trying to get pregnant. Denis still remembers the first time they had sex in the new house.

"Tell me to do it," he said.

She looked him dead in the eyes and said, "Please come inside me. Make me pregnant."

He replayed those words for months. The way she looked at him, the command in her voice, the love. She'd never spoken to him like that before.

6

The four of them went out on Denis's boat. They planned to cruise around, eventually making their way to the Onshore Café, where they would eat what Denis assured Carl was the best surf-n-turf in the whole state of North Carolina. Elena and Shari called Denis and Carl "the boys." Carl opened the cooler he brought with him, showing Denis an assortment of bottled beers, and winked in a way meant to be conspiratorial, but which looked idiotic to Denis, though he managed a smile at the beer for Carl.

Jane was at home with the babysitter, Laura, a seventeen-year-old girl from the neighborhood who had been offered a scholarship to Duke already but whose parents wanted her to learn responsibility by earning some of her own spending money. Elena told Shari how she wasn't sure what she'd do when Laura went off to college.

Carl talked about investment opportunities. "You know, you could be making some real money—not that you don't do fine—but I mean *real* money, if you bought in on some businesses."

"Also a way to lose real money." Denis looked ahead of them on the lake, holding the steering wheel with one hand and sipping a beer.

"Oh, sure, I've lost plenty," Carl said, "but if you're smart like I've been, you make a hundred times more than you lose."

Denis had never considered owning businesses or property. He suddenly felt like a country bumpkin, happy to get his little share of the pie just because it was a slightly bigger piece than he had before. He was thinking about ways to make his money grow when he saw a boat zigzagging in the distance.

Denis and Carl watched as the boat approached, admiring its sleek shape and the clean rumble of the engine. Then Denis saw the boat was headed at them. He gripped the steering wheel, but he didn't change course, unable to guess where the oncoming boat's zigzags would take it. He hit his horn, gave three sharp bursts. The boat veered starboard at the last instant. As the boat passed, close enough to spray them with water from its wake, Denis saw that the three women on board were naked. The man steering the boat stood at the wheel, shirtless and tanned, muscular and tall like a basketball player.

"Well, now," Carl said in an exaggerated Texan drawl, "would ya look at that?"

Elena and Shari had been talking and drinking their wine coolers. They came to see what the commotion was about. The three girls waved, unashamed. Denis walked down to the cooler and grabbed a beer, acting as calm as he knew how. He twisted the top off and drank, looking over the bottle at the girls receding in the distance.

"Looks like they're having fun," Shari said.

"That sonuvabitch is the one going to be having some fun," Carl said and laughed. "Must be that boat. Hey, Denis, you got to get yourself a bigger boat, and then we can really begin to have some parties out here on the lake."

Denis watched Elena rub the fabric of her shorts and twist her knee slightly inward, a little-girl gesture, probably picked up from Jane. He was struck by how long he'd known Elena. He'd known her since he was in grade school and she was just a classmate who lived down the road, a partner for riding bikes or playing board games. I've probably seen her do that a thousand times. She's been doing that since we were kids. It's not Jane she got it from; Jane's gotten it from her.

Elena said something quietly to Shari, but Denis missed it.

"What was that, honey?" Denis asked and grinned.

"Nothing," she said. But the way she and Shari looked at each other, he knew she had said something he hadn't been meant to hear. He looked to Shari for help, doofus grin still in place, but she just winked at him.

"Don't you think it'd be fun to be that kind of girl, though?" Shari said to Elena, and nodded her head in the direction the nice boat had gone. "Carefree, crazy, doing what you want?"

Elena shook her head and laughed, scrunched her face up at the implausible thought.

7

Denis met Elena when they were in the third grade, and as the family story goes (though Denis can't remember if it's true or not) when he came home from the first day of school and his mother asked how he liked the third grade, he responded that he loved it because he'd seen the prettiest girl ever.

When they began dating in high school, after years of

flirting in school and summer Bible study, Denis walked down the halls with pride, and the other boys stared at him with open envy when he kissed Elena between classes or sat holding her hand at lunch. She had grown into a girl reminiscent of models in magazines or movie actresses— her skin slightly olive, like her Greek grandfather's, and the effortless perfection of her body the envy of all her girlfriends.

But even more than her beauty, Denis loved her because she was the only other person he knew as dedicated as he was to getting out of rural North Carolina. They'd sit in the Waffle House, holding hands under the table, sipping coffee and fantasizing about what all they would do. Even then he knew he wanted to be a lawyer. He saw the law as the great equalizer. Anyone with a law degree can become rich no matter where he started, Denis thought. And he liked the high-mindedness of the law. And he liked the power of it. He'd read about the law bringing down Senators and Presidents, and he'd heard of farm boys who, after studying law, now owned mansions. The Great Equalizer. That was his secret name for the law, and though he knew it wasn't perfect, he also knew it was his best shot at making something of himself which, aside from marrying Elena one day, was all that mattered to him.

And Elena, who was the star Spanish student at Hickory High, planned on majoring in Spanish and international business. This was the early nineties, and everyone was talking about Free Trade and the future of business in Central and South America.

"I can translate for your law firm," she might say.

"And we'll have a beach house and a mountain house," he might respond.

"Will you take me to Japan? I've always wanted to go there."

"We'll see the whole world," he'd say, "one hotel room at a time." Elena would smack his arm, pretending to be offended, then turn her head and look at him through her fallen hair.

8

But now Denis is watching Elena cry as he puts his arm around her black-clad shoulder. He hates to see her in so much pain. This woman, my wife . . . He tries to imagine what life would be like without her but can't. He looks around at the people gathered and realizes he doesn't know many of them. But he knows Elena; he knows her because so much of their lives are the same and have been for decades. He pulls her closer to him, and she turns her face and rests it on his shoulder. "Denis," she says and squeezes the fine fabric of his suit jacket.

9

It soon became a habit for the couples to go out together. They got together every weekend except when Jane had a sporting event or Elena insisted on driving to Hickory to visit with their families. It was a Saturday afternoon and Carl had invited Denis over for a few games of golf. Carl and Shari lived in a golfing community on the edge of town.

Denis made fun of the street names as he and Elena drove through the neighborhood. Three Wood Drive, Caddy Lane, Nine Iron Avenue, Green Street. Jane was in the backseat, making her dolls have a conversation about the weather. "It is a beautiful day," said Barbie. "You are a beautiful day," said Ken. Denis looked over his shoulder at Jane, then to Elena.

"Would you like to have a house over here some day?"

"But we just renovated the upstairs last year."

"I don't mean now. I mean someday."

"I like our house just fine."

"Yeah, I know, but I'm a full partner now at the firm, and money isn't any issue. You know that, right?"

"I know. But I like our house. These houses are bigger, but they don't have the lake."

10

At the graveyard, his mother is holding a tissue to her face, but he doesn't see any tears. She is flabby. Her clothes are cheap, from the Wal-Mart near her house. He only cares about his wife and daughter, and now his daughter is dead. She is completely, irrevocably dead. He can't look at his mother any longer so he looks at Elena, at the perfect curve of her back, the real tears on her cheeks.

11

Denis turned in his mother's driveway and took in the smallness of her house. This had been his childhood home, where everything was huge in memory—counters head-high, ceilings unreachable. The steps on the front porch were steep to his little-boy legs. Now they were three small steps he would take in one jaunty hop. The front door seemed barely wide enough for Elena to get through.

Martha—his mother's decades-long friend, practically a member of the family—was drinking instant coffee at the kitchen table when his mother ushered them inside. The way Martha looked at Denis and then inspected Elena, he knew she had been invited over just to see how he'd grown up, how the wayward son had returned. This would be a tedious visit. After the usual back and forth of introductions, false compliments, and a few saccharine memories, all of which Denis could barely stand to listen to, his mother looked to Elena and said, "Oh, did you bring them pictures of the house?"

Denis looked at Elena. He'd heard nothing about pictures. He didn't know that his wife and his mother had spoken since the move. He tried to catch Elena's eye, but she wouldn't meet his.

"Yes, they're right here in my bag," she said. She reached into her turquoise leather handbag and produced a small package from the one-hour photo place in the mall. Denis's mother and Martha began ogling over the photos of the house and of Lake Norman.

"They live on the water," she said to Martha. "Got a boat and everything."

Denis didn't like to hear his mother speak with such pride about him. She didn't even know who he was anymore. How could she be proud of him?

Elena was pregnant with Jane at the time, but they hadn't told anyone yet. They'd just found out themselves the previous week. Denis dreaded having to hear his mother coo and giggle with delight at having a grandchild. He left the three of them to look over the photos. Outside, standing on the porch, he looked out over the expanse of trees and mountains to the east. I'm from here; such a strange thought.

His brothers were down in the barn working on his mother's pick-up truck. He figured he'd go down and say hello. It seemed the brotherly thing to do, and walking down the sparsely graveled road to the barn made him feel like a boy again. He kicked a plastic pop-bottle lid in front of him on his way, losing it in the grass just as he got to the barn.

"Well, look who we have here," Jimmy said, and Denis thought how stupid his brother sounded, like a caricature of himself from a comedy skit making fun of rednecks.

"Yes, indeed-y," said Tom. "Yes, sir, indeed. Why, it's our little brother." Tom hung his grease-blackened rag on the side-view mirror.

"Cut the shit, guys. I'm back to visit Mom, and I want this to be nice. I don't need your tweedle-dumb and tweedle-fucking-dumber act, okay?"

All his life, Denis had done nothing but cower in front of his brothers. As a child they picked on him, and in high school, they'd come home drunk and toss his books around or ask Elena whether she wanted to take a ride down by the creek with a couple of real men.

"Now give me a hug and tell me you're happy to see me, or I'll just walk back up to the house and be gone." He looked at each of them in turn, waiting for their decision.

"You sure you're not worried about dirtying that nice shirt of yours," Jimmy asked.

"Yeah, and look at them shoes," Tom added. "Hey, those're the kind shit don't stick to, right?"

They both laughed.

Denis turned and walked back toward the house.

"Aw, wittle Denis is mad," Jimmy said.

"What?" Tom said. "Can't take a joke?" But Denis didn't respond, just kept walking.

Back in the house, Denis told Elena to get her things. "We're leaving," he said. She looked at him blankly. "Get up," he said. "Let's go."

Martha put her hand to her mouth. Elena looked at Denis's mother bewildered, apologizing, as she grabbed her purse and followed Denis outside.

"What's going on?"

"Just get in the car, Elena," he said. "Please."

His mother was standing on the porch mouth working for something to say, until finally, "You forgot your pictures."

"Keep them," Denis said, holding back none of the acid in his voice.

12

It was at a birthday party for one of Elena's sorority sisters, Denis doesn't remember which, that they had met Emiliano. This was their junior year at UNC. Emiliano was from Spain, studying abroad here in America for a year, and as a native speaker of Spanish he was often invited to Spanish Department parties. They were introduced and Emiliano spoke Spanish with Elena. Denis stood there, smiling dumbly, waiting for them to revert to English. Elena laughed at something Emiliano said, and Denis smiled bigger and looked at her, and then at Emiliano.

After Emiliano had moved on to another cluster of people, Denis asked, "So, what were you and Rico Suave talking about there?"

"Just how great the party is and stuff. Can't you understand anything going on?"

Denis was back-rowing it in his Spanish class at the time, barely pulling a B, and that was with hours of help from Elena. It drove him crazy, not being able to learn it. He had hoped that he could be fluent so Elena and he could speak Spanish together. There was something romantic about that idea to him. But, despite perfect grades in every other subject, his brain just couldn't make sense of a foreign language.

A week later he saw Emiliano and Elena walking together out of a coffee shop on Franklin Street, where all the UNC students hung out. He didn't confront them, but that night, he asked Elena about it.

"He's helping me with my Spanish," she said.

"Yeah?"

"Yeah."

"Well, just keep it at that."

"What's that supposed to mean?"

"Exactly what it means."

One night, a month later, they were in her dorm room. Denis began playfully undoing her pants. She froze, pushed him away, and turned on the light. Her roommate's pot-leaf poster looked so ridiculous on the opposite wall, and all Denis wanted to do was have sex.

"What's wrong," he said, trying to sound concerned.

"We can't."

"Why not?" he asked.

"There's something I have to tell you."

It was Emiliano, as he had known it would eventually be Emiliano, that man from so far away, a place nothing like Hickory or even Chapel Hill, North Carolina. She loved him more than ever, she insisted. "This is a good thing," she said. "It made me see how much you matter to me."

"You sucking some other guy's dick is a good thing for me?"

She hugged herself to him, but he kept his arms pressed to his sides. He knew he wouldn't break things off with her, but he didn't want to talk about it, didn't want to be asked to forgive her. He just wanted the whole thing over with so he could pretend it never happened.

13

Standing beside her now in the cemetery—all these people around, the bare trees behind the preacher—Denis wonders what ever happened to Emiliano. It seems funny that he ever entered their lives. It's like a story about someone else. Denis can't put himself back in his college self. He wishes he wasn't thinking of some long-forgotten Spaniard who had fucked his wife, though the fact no longer holds any hurt for him.

14

He and Shari were driving down Tyvola Road. It was the third time they'd met, though he had hoped there would only be the first. Now the prospect of a prolonged affair was before him, and he wanted to have the strength to end it. Shari put her hand on his thigh. The weight of it sitting there was nice. He could feel the fabric of his suit pants slick against his leg. Carl was out of town, so they hadn't bothered with a hotel. Something about how Denis felt fucking another man's wife in their bed made him angry. How could Shari do that to Carl? It had been maybe the best sex of his life, or close. He smiled at the memory of it, and Shari began massaging his leg, working her way up. When he felt himself getting hard, he slapped her hand away.

"We have to stop," he said. "You know that, right?"

"Yeah."

"Come on, you have to know that."

"Okay, okay. I fucking well know it, already."

He drove on for several minutes before she put her hand back on his leg. He looked at her, and she looked at him, smiled a little apologetic smile, tilting her head downward and to the left, letting her eyes close slowly. Making sure I appreciate the gesture. But he didn't move her hand away, and he didn't stop her as she unzipped his pants. He was worried about the other cars on the road and worried briefly that he might crash. That would be a total disaster. There was a large parking lot to his right, with a huge blinking neon sign. He pushed Shari's hand away and pulled into the parking lot. When he had parked, he zipped his pants up over his uncomfortable erection and looked at her.

"I'm serious," he said.

"I know you are," she said. "But things were so nice today, weren't they?"

As they got out of the car, he looked at the neon sign. Pink's Skate Rink. What a stupid thing to name a place. Inside they sat in the farthest corner and drank diet sodas. Shari told him about how the golf course in her neighborhood was being re-done by some famous landscape architect. She made a joke about shrubbery shaped as giraffes and dolphins.

(Now, Denis looks at her, here at his daughter's funeral, and is sorry that he didn't laugh at her joke. He's sorry he never called her again, but he hadn't had any choice. He misses her sense of humor. He turns toward Elena, making sure she hasn't noticed him staring at Shari.)

15

When Officer Jenkins called, the slow way he said *Mr. Seldin* and breathed out, pushing a wind of static through the phone, let Denis know it was bad. Denis waited to hear about how Jane had been repeatedly raped and buried in a garbage bag. Or chopped to bits by some multi-state serial killer. Or...

"Some kids found her," Officer Jenkins said. "They had snuck into a drainage ditch to smoke a joint and drink beers." He told Denis that the kids had smelled her before they saw her. Then he apologized. "I'm sorry, Mr. Seldin, I didn't—"

"No, I want to know everything."

"Maybe you'd better get down to the coroner's office, Mr. Seldin," he said. "We can't even be sure yet it's definitely her."

"You sounded pretty sure a minute ago," Denis said.

"You want the number down at the coroner's? I can give it to you."

"Yeah, I'd like the number, if that's not too much to ask."

Denis grabbed one of Elena's post-it note pads and wrote down the number. The post-it note was one with pastel hearts in the upper corners and a flowery landscape along the bottom. He stared at the post-it note and his handwriting. The numbers looked like hieroglyphics with those sky-hearts floating above them, alien and absurd. Denis put his hand on the counter and eased himself slowly to the floor and sat on the cold linoleum of the kitchen, clutching the post-it note.

He tried to figure out what he would tell Elena. Officer Jenkins had said she'd drowned, likely fell in and hit her head or went into shock from the cold water. At least Jane wasn't raped. And don't people go into shock when they drown in such cold water? Don't even feel any pain at all? He'd heard that somewhere. At least there was that. He promised himself he wouldn't Google *drowning* or *death by drowning* or *pain + drowning*.

He and Elena went to see the body. It was water-bloated, making her seem larger than she was in life, her features softened and sloppy. There wasn't much to do. They signed the paperwork. The State would pay for an autopsy to eliminate the possibility of foul play, though preliminary results indicated none. The body would be transported to a funeral home of their choice, they were told, which sent Elena into a spasm of tears.

He dreamed about Jane's body floating in their bathtub several nights in a row after seeing her.

16

And so the story had died on TV. Mystery solved. Not a murder or kidnapping, nothing exciting, just another dead girl. Next story. Next. Denis turned on the TV for days expecting to see more about his daughter's disappearance, but it was never mentioned again. Every political rally, every car wreck, every family-dog-saves-kid-from-drowning story was an insult to Jane's memory. Next. It got to where he couldn't watch TV at all. If Jane's death wasn't news, nothing was.

17

Elena holds her face in one hand and leans against Denis, holding onto his shoulder for support. Elena's mother and his brothers stand behind them. Elena's father is talking to the preacher, but Denis can't hear what they're saying. The grass is being stamped down, Denis notices. That can't be good for the grass, having so many people trample all over it. Cousins, friends, Jane's teachers and friends and basketball coach, Denis's brothers, mostly people Denis doesn't care about, walk past them. *I'm so sorry*, they say to Denis. *I'm so sorry*, they say to Elena. *I'm sorry*, everyone is saying. He just wants to be at home, lying in bed silent with Elena, saying nothing but holding her, the only person in the world.

18

It had been an April evening, and he wondered what Elena and Jane were doing. He decided on the drive home that he'd take them out to dinner somewhere nice. "It's such a beautiful day," he would say when he came in the door. "Let's celebrate."

But when he got home, Elena was sitting in her spot on the couch in the living room, but the TV wasn't on. The lights were all off and she was sitting there doing nothing. She knows, Denis thought. Shari had finally confessed. He had known it was coming but had pretended it wasn't going to happen.

"What are you doing in here?"

"Fuck you."

"Hey, what's that about?" Denis asked and clicked on a lamp. Elena looked at the lamp as if she'd never noticed they had a lamp in that particular corner.

"Where's Jane?" he asked, though he could hear her playing upstairs.

"Don't worry, I'm not going to divorce you," Elena said.

"Honey, I'm sorry."

"And Jane deserves a family."

"I'm so sorry," Denis said.

"Don't apologize. Just don't," she said, and he thought she might cry, but then her voice changed. "Everyone makes mistakes, Denis," she said calmly, almost wisely, as if she could look at the human error he'd made and even pity it. "I know how easy it can be." She looked at him and smiled a sad little smile. "So, now we're even."

"It wasn't like that."

"But you have to stop seeing her," she said. "You don't even get to call her to explain why. And I never—I mean *never*—want to talk about this again. Do you understand?"

Denis sat down beside her and took both of her hands in his. As he looked into Elena's face and wanted to kiss her moist cheeks and eyelids, he heard Jane upstairs, jumping up and down on her bed, screeching each time she went up in the air.

"Yes," he said, "I do."

THE LONG WALK HOME

As the plane made its troubled descent, Reynolds' leg began beeping. It had been a turbulent flight, and the plane was unusually crowded. Dried sweat, stale cabin air, and the bad tempers of passengers who'd been confined too long. People had noticed his Army fatigues and duffel bag when he boarded in Newark, the way people always notice a soldier in civilian surroundings. Now the passengers near Reynolds were looking at him, at first to find the source of the beeping and then with growing anxiety. One man seemed about to jump out of his chair and either attack or flee to the other end of the plane. Reynolds tried a confused smile and shrugged his shoulders, and when that didn't stop the stares, he knocked on his prosthetic leg hard enough for everyone around to hear.

"New leg," he said. "Battery must be low."

He knew as soon as he'd said it that most people don't think of prosthetic legs as having batteries – he hadn't either, until the doctor in the Mannheim military hospital explained his leg to him – but he didn't want to give a lecture on prosthetics to these assholes. He shrugged his shoulders again for the nervous passengers and tried a little laugh, to let them know he had a sense of humor. Terrorists don't have a sense of humor. Crazy, crippled soldiers about to snap and blow up a plane don't have a sense of humor. The other passengers slowly turned away but didn't return to their conversations.

In the airport, Reynolds sat on the floor of the carpeted tunnel of the baggage claim, next to the only electric outlet he could find, his leg recharging. A boy more or less his age, but with tattoos of cartoonish demons and grotesquely large-breasted women covering his arms, had his laptop plugged into the same outlet. Reynolds was impressed the boy didn't react more severely when he plugged in his leg. Instead, he nodded, as if saying, *Cool leg, man.* The tattoos were such saturated colors, they seemed to jump off the boy's skin in an orgy of fangs and outsized anatomy. Reynolds realized how long it had been since he'd been laid, or even been near a woman who spoke his language. Hedonism, where he'd been, had consisted of pizza night or an old sun-bleached copy of *Victoria's Secret.*

He thought of calling his father, though he didn't want to stay at his father's house. He considered a hotel room. He could afford to stay at one long enough to find an apartment, though that would be a waste of money—but still, maybe just for the night? The lighting and the thin carpet of the airport seemed stagey, a façade from behind which a world of gunfire and sweeping sandstorms could suddenly emerge. Anything could happen. Watching the conveyor belt scrape its way round, luggage that belonged to unknown people bumping against other luggage, Reynolds played with the idea that there might be a bomb in one—a thought that oddly pleased him. All these people dead. After the fifth try, he gave up on reaching his father. He leaned his head against the smooth hardness of the wall and tapped his fingers on his leg as it recharged.

He scrolled through his phone for old friends he could stay with. Tom Sloan: Gone to University of Virginia. Jeremy Shields: Ohio State. Brett Lowell: Davidson College. Brett had been his best friend through middle and high school. They hadn't spoken since Reynolds enlisted, and that conversation had been likely their last ever.

"How can you sign up to be a thug for imperial forces?"

Brett had asked, the stark black tattoos up and down his arms making him look even angrier than he was (so much more intense than the cartoon world of the boy beside Reynolds right now). Brett had declared himself a socialist at age fourteen, went to protests in places like Seattle and D.C. and New York. Reynolds had never much cared for politics.

"And your grades are good enough to get into a good school. Taking a year off to work, I can see. But now you want to do this?" Reynolds had visited Brett a few times at school, and they would go into Charlotte to score some weed and bring it back to Davidson to party with. Brett had been accepted to Duke and Wake Forest, but Davidson had offered him a full scholarship, so he'd gone.

"Don't you think you'd do your country much more good as a doctor or engineer than as a murderer?" Brett went on. Reynolds was never the talker Brett was, so he let him have his say. It was hard for Reynolds to remember his retort. Probably something like *Fuck you* and not much more. But despite his inarticulateness, Reynolds felt himself to be right—that there was a deeper morality that Brett, for all his talk of equality and revolution, missed. Now, looking down at his prosthetic, Reynolds wondered if Brett had been right. Wondered if there was such a thing as right.

Outside, he looked for a cab, thinking of how he didn't need his father's money anymore—his wallet was flush and his bank account was full from living off the Army for his two years in-country. A man in a janitor's uniform and with one enormous dreadlock slung over a shoulder approached him. His eyes were polished cue balls rimmed with pink.

"Cabbie all gone, man," he said. "They on strike. You want to buy her?"

He held up a doll, an Indian girl with dark braids down her back. One of its marble eyes swung by a worn thread, yellow stuffing blooming from the socket. It was moth-eaten and stamped with mud. The man's face reminded Reynolds of a housewife in Qatar whose husband he'd been ordered to detain. She was veiled from head to toe, and all he could see were those eyes, wet with accusation and plea. She thrust money at him, a fistful of coins worth maybe half an American dollar. Her husband struggled in his binds, and a soldier brought his boot down on the man's jaw. A tooth splintered and blood dribbled forth.

"All right," Reynolds said to the man with the Indian doll, pulling out his wallet and handing him the first bill he found. The man winked and then trotted away, in pursuit of other game, leaving Reynolds on the curb with an Indian princess under his arm and the sky streaking purple and red to the west. In a minute, he'd have to begin the long walk down the narrow strip of highway, but for now he sat there thinking of the past and lightly hugging the doll to his chest.

Two years out of high school, Reynolds had enlisted in the army, hoping to better himself—to flush all that was flimsy and unconfirmed in him. His father, the chair of the political science department at the University of North Carolina at Charlotte, seemed happy to see Reynolds go. Since his mother had died and his father had remarried, Reynolds felt like an outsider in his father's house. He hadn't expected tears, but relief to see him leave was too much. That day, he decided to hate his father. He wanted to tell him that he'd lost his son forever but didn't.

The Army singled him out for its Arabic interpreter program, since he had spent his junior year of high school in Jordan where his father was doing a faculty exchange program with Yarmouk University. Still now when he thought of Jordan, he could smell the eucalyptus and see the side-winding sand made sinewy by the evening light. He loved the Arabic language, its lilting song and throaty halts, the elegant calligraphic scrawl of the writing. They lived in the city of Irbid, an unimpressive place where Reynolds quickly grew bored, but he identified heavily with his father then and wanted to please him by doing well in school. He convinced himself that if he could perfect his Arabic, his father would be impressed and respect him; instead, his father was angry when, one evening, Reynolds spent hours speaking with the dinner guests, Jordanian professors at the university, in flawed but impressive Arabic.

"Your son is very masterful with the Arabic language," an economics professor said. Reynolds smiled and looked to his father.

"Well, he never stops talking, so no wonder."

Reynolds heard annoyance in his father's voice, which he was accustomed to, but it was the tinge of envy that unseated him. He stared at his father for a moment then went to his room without saying anything further to the guests.

The recruiting officials assured him he'd go far. It pleased Reynolds that they were so happy, pleased him that he would facilitate communication. But he was sent to a spread of desert where the sun flexed angry and red in the sky. He was assigned to an encampment of yellow tarps where he showered and bunked with a hundred sullen boys from the trailer parks of Appalachia, the tenements of Baltimore, the salt of Utah. He wanted Brett to meet these boys, so he would know they were not mere murderers.

No one around him seemed to care or acknowledge that a massacre was going on. He had expected disease—AIDS, malaria, some lingering and tenacious form of the plague—and those he found, but what he had not been prepared for was the illogic of war. People were starving in hovels; water and rice shipments had been cordoned off. The ground was pocked with landmines, and he had seen a boy his age dragging the stringy stump of a leg in the dirt, an image that would come to him later as he himself lay in his hospital bed, waiting to be fitted for his prosthetic. The boy looked up and met Reynolds's eyes in a terrified prayer. Reynolds turned away. Not two weeks later, they had seen a mother strung naked on a wooden pole, her two sons looking on as militiamen sodomized her. When they were sated, they took a straight razor and stripped the skin of her back until bone poked through like a smile. Reynolds lifted his gun in his chalk-white hands, but a sergeant stopped him.

"Those are our allies," he said.

Reynolds wanted to say something, but what was there to say?

Reynolds gathered his things and prepared for the long walk home. He still had his keys, and maybe his father wouldn't be there. The stuffed body of the doll sagged pleasantly under his arm. Why hadn't he gone to college after high school instead?

Then he remembered her, Laura Goetz, who had been his date for senior prom, an achingly pale girl with dozens of finger-length braids. Her accompanying him to prom was one of the triumphs of his teen years. He took a breath and dialed her number. A gravelly female voice answered. "I told you not to call here anymore." It was a slurry voice he didn't recognize. Maybe Laura had moved.

"It's Reynolds Fisher," he said. He heard a faint rustling, the creaking of something like bedsprings. "I'm calling for Laura Goetz. Is this the right number?"

"Reynolds?" she said. "Why are you calling me?"

He nearly hung up.

"I'm sorry," she said. "My god, I'm such a bitch. I didn't mean that. It's just such a surprise is all."

A half hour later, a Lincoln with one green door, one brown door, and a crumpled hood squeaked to a stop in front of the terminal. He tossed his bags in the back seat and slid in. "You saved my life," he said and got into the car, embarrassed of his leg. He had learned to walk gracefully enough, but there were still certain motions that made him feel like a poorly functioning cyborg from a B sci-fi movie. To Laura's credit, she was neither staring nor pointedly not looking. She struck match after match, trying to light a cigarette. Her face was swollen and blotched, with waxy, gray pockets under her eyes. The corners of her mouth, once dimpled and smooth, now sagged.

"You look good," he said.

"I look like shit."

They drove through a wet canopy of woods, the moon flickering in a hazy distance. The dry swaying grass between the trees had something of a rippling desert to it in that light. Reynolds set the doll on the dashboard between them, and Laura eyed it briefly. Her face beamed a strange happiness at the doll. The radio crackled, but she made no move to change the station. Laura took a sharp turn and the doll fell, but Reynolds' hand shot out and caught it, placed it back in its seat on the dashboard. He was pleased with how quickly his hand had moved, that he hadn't really thought to catch the doll, just simply did. He felt very soldierly, even though he knew he'd accomplished no great deed of heroism. In town, a few cars crawled lazily in the buzzing streetlight, but otherwise it was as soupy and silent as the woods they'd been in a minute before.

"Where can I drop you?"

"My dad's, I suppose."

"You suppose?"

He traced a finger in the dust on the dash, studied it in the honey-colored light of the closed shops.

"You want to come to my place for a while?" she asked. "I could use some company."

She lived in her parent's basement which had to be entered through the garage. Inside, a bed draped with a princess curtain was littered with stained quilts and magazine clippings. The phone was ringing, but she ignored it.

"I'm making a collage," she said, clearing the bed.

There was a picture of Laura and a shaggy-haired man on her bedside table; the man's face looked familiar, but Reynolds couldn't place it. There were bottles scattered across the carpet, in various stages of emptiness. A few were broken, their jigsaw pieces stacked in a pale blue salad bowl. One bottle had spilled on the carpet, amber liquid trickling from its mouth. Laura grabbed a towel from the bathroom and spread it over the spill. She stepped on the towel and rubbed it around.

"A thousand apologies." She smiled, and for a minute he could sense the compact grace still in her flesh. "Okay, maybe three hundred. Want some vodka?"

She took a sip and tumbled back on the bed, holding the bottle out to him. He took a cautious swallow and felt the burn rush down his throat. Something warm and sour rose in his mouth, and he looked around for a sink. Laura pointed to the bathtub. As he knelt to drink he felt her eyes on him and heard her easy laughter. The phone was ringing again.

"Aren't you going to answer that?"

She shook her head. "Tell me about it. Over there, I mean."

"I'd rather not." He felt that words would trivialize what he'd seen, and besides, she wouldn't understand. The phone was still ringing, endless and hysterical. "Jesus Christ," he said.

"Was it that bad?"

"Worse." It sounded like a good thing to say, restrained and mysterious, as if he was showing her an uncommon kindness by sparing her the details.

They lay on their backs, passing the bottle in loose, companionable silence. A fly crawled across the ceiling and disappeared into a crack.

"Sometimes I get so lonely here," she said.

"I know what you mean," he said. "I didn't have many friends over there."

"But then I think of all the fucked up things I've done, and I wonder if I'm not exactly where I need to be."

"Lance Davies," he said, remembering the name of the man in the photo with her. He'd heard she had dated Lance after graduation. "Did you," Reynolds began, but stopped, suddenly unable to care about small-town romances.

"Did I fuck him?" She giggled and let the empty bottle drop. It bounced off the mattress and landed with a soft thud on a delicately blue sweater on the floor. She unsnapped her bra; there was a yellow and gray bruise the size of a fist on her left breast. "I married him."

"It's him that keeps calling?" he asked.

"Does it matter?" She took his hand and raised it to her

bruise. His palm neatly eclipsed the mark, leaving only healthy skin. She began tugging down her panties. The doll he'd given her was sitting primly on a shelf, its sprung eye hanging from the socket and resting between its legs. He wanted to put it back in place but didn't.

Laura unzipped him and tugged his fatigues off, careful of his prosthetic. She rubbed the inside of his thighs, letting the hand on his left leg wander as far as just past his knee, but the one on his right leg stopped at the prosthetic's beginning. She pulled his briefs off, again careful.

"Do you leave it on?" she asked.

"I've not really had a chance one way or the other," he said. "Not yet."

"Let's leave it on," she said and took his half-hard penis into her mouth. When she had gotten him very hard, she said, "Now my turn," and flopped over onto her back.

As Laura pushed his face into her sweaty tangle of pubic hair, he tried not to think of the dead boy he'd found in a gutter, a bullet wound in his jaw and cheek. A fly had crawled out of the hole where the boy's eye had been, and Reynolds doubled over and vomited in the street. Matthew, a quiet boy from northern Minnesota—almost Canada, as he put it— offered him a page of newsprint to wipe his mouth. He tried not to think of Matthew either, who lost both of his legs and his balls to a roadside bomb three weeks later, a bomb their unit would have known about had Reynolds not fucked up the interrogation of several captives. They spoke a variation of the Gulf dialect he was particularly weak with because he found it unappealing. Reynolds was disgusted at himself; he hadn't gotten one damned thing right in his entire life. At least I can still get laid, unlike Matthew, he thought, half-sick and half-amused.

He reminded himself to focus, to simply be here—and *now*. He pumped into Laura, telling himself he liked the animal in their noises, their immediate and real proof of life. But he kept thinking of starving people and the military-issue condoms in his backpack over by the door. He wondered how many men Laura had been with and what diseases she might have, but this only made him harder and made him thrust more violently into her. He looked at her breasts, thinking how nice they were, then saw her bruise. Lance Davies' face flashed in his mind, and he closed his eyes. Someone needed to tell Lance to leave her alone. Someone needed to tell him there would be consequences if he didn't.

"Where do you want me to come?"

"It doesn't matter," Laura said.

He collapsed on top of her and lay there, breathing and sweating, feeling like he wanted to kill something. He hugged her to him and knew they would do this many more times. She looked at him, and he thought he saw something like happiness in her face. The image of them dressed up—all those years ago, just children—came to him, and he felt a sense of knowing that comes with living the unexpected. He squeezed her, wanting to reassure her that he was good and wasn't leaving and was already feeling the first tingles of what people call love. But the phone rang again, destroying everything. Reynolds jumped out of bed, landing deftly on his left foot then balancing himself with his prosthetic. He stared at the phone, listening to it ring and ring and ring. This time he answered. He knew exactly what to say.

EL PUEBLO DE NUESTRA SEÑORA
LA REINA DE LOS ÁNGELES

I met Bobbie the day Dean shot a Mexican out in front of our trailer. Bobbie and her mom had just moved into Whispering Grove earlier that week. They had the nice sky-blue trailer down at the end, near the steps where I sometimes liked to skateboard. Bobbie had on a tight white T and cut-off denims that showed off her summer tan, and I tried not to look at her, but she was wearing a red bra she knew everyone could see through her shirt.

Dean was talking over the gathered crowd, repeating his version of events like he figured that by saying it over and over it'd become the official story people told. Thing is, that works a lot of times. And since the Mexican didn't speak very good English, just sat in the gravel of our driveway holding his arm, he didn't get much of a say into how things had gone. Blood leaked through his fingers and his face was vacant, like he was a hundred miles from all of the commotion.

"...and this *hombre* here was climbing in my window, so I shot him right where he stood," Dean was saying. The way the Mexican just sat there as though this little trifle was the least of the worries he'd seen in life made me on his side more than Dean's. Not that Dean was a bad guy. He was really nice to Sandy, my mom. He paid bills and even showed up with flowers and a six pack after they had an argument.

41

Sandy called him a real romantic, and I had to admit he was better than some of the guys she'd dated.

Bobbie walked over to me. "Your dad is some kind of hero, huh?"

It took me a second to realize she was talking about Dean. My dad is no hero. You can believe me on that one. "Yeah, I guess so," I said, "but he's not my dad. That's Dean."

Bobbie popped her gum and scratched at a mosquito bite on the inside of her thigh as she took Dean in. She stood there like she expected more conversation out of me. I thought of several more things to say, but they all sounded stupid when I played them in my head, so I kept quiet. Dean was still waving the gun around, jabbing it in the air to punctuate what he was saying. And all the while the Mexican just sat there.

The cops finally showed up and took him away. They told Dean they needed his gun for evidence, but you could tell they figured this was a pretty straightforward case. Several men from the crowd—men dressed in oil-stained jeans and torn shirts—told the cops they'd seen the whole thing and that it'd gone down just the way Dean was saying it did, even though some of them had shown up after I did, and I hadn't gotten there in time to see anything. But I didn't say anything. I figured, whatever, fuck it, and went inside, taking one more look at Bobbie as I went.

That night I had to get out. All Dean would do was retell the story Sandy and I'd heard a dozen times. He had a few beers in him and just kept talking talking talking. I grabbed my skateboard and went out the backdoor. I was olleying down the steps at the end of Whispering Grove when I saw Bobbie beside her trailer. I wanted to land the olley real smooth but instead slammed into the pavement, jarring my noggin a bit. When I opened my eyes, Bobbie was standing over me, one foot planted on either side of my hips. In the street's lighting, the tent of her skirt made a shadow I couldn't see through, so I looked up into her face.

"I stole some of my mom's Valium," she said. "Wanna do them with me?"

I suggested we go down by the tracks where I had a place I liked to go when I smoked up.

"I hate this place," Bobbie said and threw a rock at a bottle sitting by the tracks. I thought she meant my spot. "Why'd mom have to move us from L.A.? I mean, what the fuck is in Greensboro, North K-K-Karolina?"

It was hard to imagine Bobbie in a Beverly Hills mansion, almost as hard as imagining her in a trailer park.

"And my old boyfriend, Lizard, won't even talk to me on the phone. He says he doesn't want to talk to some country bumpkin."

We lay there a minute or so, her talking about how great this guy Lizard was. She showed me a tattoo of a red dragon she had on her upper stomach. "He gave that one to me," she said. "My mom doesn't even know I have it." Lizard was this nineteen-year-old guy she hung out with back in L.A. until her mom decided he was too old to be around Bobbie. I was trying hard to think of something to say that'd make her happy she was here.

"You ever notice how people say they're going to *do* pills if it's not their prescription, but they *take* it if it is?" I like little things like that, things we say that seem insignificant but really tell us a lot about what we're doing. Sandy tells me I should major in psychology if I go to college someday.

But Bobbie looked at me like I was the strangest damned thing she'd ever seen. "Yeah, I guess so. Never thought of it that way," she offered. I was disappointed I'd said it then, and of a sudden my little observation didn't seem so hawk-eyed.

Bobbie lay on her back and said how good she felt from the Valium. I couldn't feel a thing, but I acted like I did as soon as she lay down. I went to one elbow beside her and told her I knew what she meant. "I just wish we had some beer," was my only complaint. I thought about whether she'd let me finger her. She seemed like the kind of girl who would, if you did things right.

"So what's L.A. all about?"

She stared up at the night sky and rattled off, "*El Pueblo de Nuestra Señora la Reina de Los Angeles.*"

"What's that?"

"It's L.A.'s real name. It means, The City of Our Lady the Queen of the Angels. That's nice, don't you think?" Something about it was. Like a fantasy kingdom, or from the Bible maybe.

"Did you live in a Beverly Hills mansion?"

"My dad was a car salesman. Until his extra-curriculars caught up with him and he got AIDS from some junkie slut," she said. "He's dead now."

"Oh."

"Are you going to kiss me or not?" Bobbie asked, irritated, as though she'd been waiting hours for me to get around to it.

She was a good kisser. The one smart thing my dad ever said was that you can tell more about how you feel for a girl when you kiss her than you can any other way. Somehow all the things you pretended to feel are replaced by the things you really feel, if you're paying attention enough to notice.

After a while it was time for Bobbie to go home, so I walked her back and kissed her once more before she ran up to her trailer. I watched her take the steps in twos. As she shut the door behind her, she turned to see if I was still there and smiled at me before the door clicked shut against those sky-blue walls. I hopped on my skateboard, gave two smooth pushes and glided, the night air whooshing by. I felt like I could do anything, like I was king of the fucking world.

When I got back home, a cop car was out front, and Dean was leaning out of the screen door jabbing his finger in the air toward a young, blond officer who looked to be about twice Dean's size and built like a German tank. Another cruiser pulled up and Dean's cousin Russell got out.

"What in hell's unholy name have you gotten yourself into here, Dean?"

Dean stopped paying attention to the blond officer and smiled to see someone he knew. "Well, well, you old bastard! It's good to be able to talk to somebody with some sense," he said as he walked down to meet Russell.

"Just get to it, Dean."

"Well, you see, I was defending my home here from a Mexican burglar earlier today..."

"...and now he's pressing charges, claiming he was coming by to get money you owe him. I know all that, Dean. That's not what I'm asking."

"What are you askin' then, Mr. Officer?" Dean spat out.

"I'm asking what you've gone and gotten yourself mixed up in this time." Russell just stood there, cold-eyed and unmoving.

Since Dean'd moved in, Russell came over from time to time. He'd check up on Sandy and me, sometimes bring a fruit basket or case of Pepsi for us. He'd look around the trailer and talk about Dean's and his family a little. I never knew why he came by, but I liked him, thought I might even become a cop some day. You never know.

"Do you have any kids?" I asked him maybe the second or third time he came over.

"Yep. Two. Shaindel and Tristan, both twelve. Twins. Lucy and me wanted to have a baby and just got more than we bargained for. Better than most people can say in life, I guess."

When he didn't offer to introduce me, I figured he didn't want his kids hanging around trailer trash, so I dropped the subject.

Dean was looking right back at Russell just as coldly. "You here to take me in? Is that how it is?"

"No. Right now, all we have is his word against yours. I'm here to serve you papers to show up in court next month and let a judge settle it." Russell handed him some official looking papers stapled sloppily on top. Dean snatched them out of his hand. "I'd advise you to get a lawyer, Dean." Russell's voice was soft for his size.

"So, are we done here, Mr. Officer? If so, take blondie over here and get the hell away from my house."

The blond officer's muscles tensed. He looked like he could tear a man's head clean off.

"Alright, John, let's get outta here," Russell said to the blond officer. "Oh, and Dean, don't go making plans to leave the state anytime soon."

Sandy had been standing just inside the screen door the whole time, hugging her arms to herself, puffing away on one of her menthols. When Dean turned to walk in, he saw her. She asked him what was going on, but he just opened the screen door and brushed by her.

Lying in bed that night, all I could think about was the feel of Bobbie. I could hear Sandy and Dean arguing in the other room. With them talking and me thinking of Bobbie, I couldn't sleep, so I just lay there in the dark, looking around my room. On my chest of drawers a snow globe Sandy had bought me when I was seven or eight glowed orange from the streetlight outside my window. It's a strange thing to admit, but I love snow globes. They're these little worlds where nothing really ever happens. I jumped up and gave it a shake, sending the slow flakes swimming, and lay back down. Little brown shadows fluttered across the wall, and I was almost able to ignore Sandy and Dean yapping away.

The next day was the first of May, and like the first of every month people called it Mother's Day, because that's when the welfare checks came in. Men who hadn't been home for weeks would suddenly be at the door with a ratty rose in hand, sons who'd dropped out of school to sell weed or work on construction sites between drunks showed up to see what was for dinner and to talk about how they just had a great job and another was surely on the way.

I wondered whether my dad was going to show up. A few months back, he'd stopped coming around, even on Mother's Day.

Sandy was at work, but Dean had the day off, so he was smoking up on the couch. I came in and sat beside him, waited to see if he would hand me the joint. Sometimes he was greedy and kept it to himself, but if I waited until he was stoned enough, he'd give me some. I asked Dean how business was. He got this conspiratorial look on his face and motioned for me to follow him back to his and Sandy's bedroom. I didn't really like going in there too much anymore, not since Dean had moved in and his things were on the walls and shelves. But I followed him and watched as he opened the closet door and pushed Sandy's dresses back to show me the four puffy, full trash bags sitting in back. I could smell what was in them before he even opened one up.

"Just look at it, would ya? Just look at that shit," he said, and I thought how later I could steal maybe as much as an ounce and he'd never notice with how much he had.

"Yeah, that there's going to be my ticket out of here. Dean Morrison wasn't meant for this kind of living. No, sir," he added, an afterthought, and looked out the window with his bloodshot eyes. "Maybe I'll take you and your mom with me. How'd you like that?"

I told him I'd like that just fine I guess, and we dropped the subject, but it got me thinking about how he had a plan and how I wanted one too. I was still thinking about it as we went back to the couch and smoked the rest of Dean's joint and then rolled another.

Sandy talked a lot about me going to college, which didn't sound bad when I considered all the drugs and girls college guys get. And maybe she was right about majoring in psychology. I took another hit and pictured myself in an office with a leather couch and a bawling lady-patient in a nice dress and dark lipstick.

"So, what's up with you and that tight little piece Bobbie? You get a taste of that punany yet?"

I was pretty stoned and couldn't figure out whether to lie or not, so I just stuck two fingers up in the air in the shape of a V and flicked my tongue between them, knowing that'd make Dean happy. He nearly fell down laughing.

After that first night, Bobbie was more or less my girlfriend you could say. I'd come over to her trailer in the afternoons when her mom was at work down at the Winn Dixie, and we'd pop valium and play Nintendo for hours. Sometimes she'd lean on my shoulder and doze for a bit. Other times we'd fool around.

It was next Mother's Day and we were sitting on her couch kissing and talking about what we wanted to be one day. We were pretty stoned, still riding high off the stuff I'd stolen from Dean. I got to thinking about far-off places where people make it rich and get what they want and are happy.

"You know, I was thinking that maybe I could do Spanish in college. Sandy is always saying how she'd have a better job if she could speak Spanish," I said. Bobbie gave me that look of hers that let me know what I was saying was stupid, but I didn't stop. I told her about how people get jobs in airports if they speak Spanish and how you're supposed to get free flights if you work there.

"Wouldn't that be cool?" I asked. "We could go anywhere we wanted."

"Pretty cool," she said and flipped on the television.

I tried to say L.A.'s name, "El pe-ebblo day…"

"El Pueblo de Nuestra Señora la Reina de los Angeles."

"Do you ever think of going back there?" I asked.

"I have to stay with Mom until I finish high school." She was going through the channels too fast for me to tell what was on, so I stopped looking at the screen and just looked at her.

"I'm thinking of moving to L.A., maybe go pro," I said and kicked my skateboard, sending a wheel spinning.

Her face brightened, and she leaned her body toward me so much it looked like something from a soap opera Sandy might watch.

"Yeah," I said. "I got it all planned out."

I could tell Bobbie was excited, so I kept lying, or not lying really, 'cause I meant every word I was saying when I said it, and I wanted to move to L.A. with her so bad. I didn't give a damn about the Stars—Carmen Electra, Tom Cruise, and all them. Fuck Tom Cruise. I just wanted me and Bobbie to lie on the beach all year round and smoke pot and maybe I could go pro, and we could get married, have some kids, do it right.

"But I'm not going to end up like my mother," Bobbie said.

"No way," I said and hugged her to me, kissed the crown

of her head like people do to kids sometimes, "we're not gonna be like any of them."

That night I woke up to screaming. Even groggy as I was, I knew it was him. I jumped from bed and slipped my jeans on, not bothering with shirt or shoes. On the way out of my room, I saw the little snow globe and grabbed it. Sandy was screaming *Get out! Get out! Get the fuck out of my fucking house!* Her voice was loud and spit-wet and scratchy. She was screaming with her eyes closed and fists pressed to her hips, I knew. That's how she always screamed at him when he decided to drop in, drunk and wanting to sleep in her bed.

"Baby, don't be like this," Dad was saying, reaching out to her with a trembling hand. The front door was open, and I could see Dad's truck parked on the grass right in front of the trailer.

I stood at the end of the hallway, squeezing the base of the snow globe so tight my hand hurt.

"He lives here now. This is his house too," Sandy was saying. "You can't be here when he gets home."

"What, I can't come see my wife and boy? You're still my wife, you know. Just 'cause you've shacked up with this sonuvabitch don't make you not my wife. You're still my wife."

Sandy slumped into him, sobbing. "Why do you do this to me?" she asked, crying into his chest. Dad put his arm around her and squeezed.

"I can't stay away from you. You know that."

Clenching the snow globe, I stared at the back of his head, where the hair was going thin, where his soft, white skin showed.

Sandy pushed against his chest hard and her face went cold. She shoved a twenty dollar bill into his hand. "Leave. Please, just leave." And I guess he heard something in her voice that I missed, because he backed away from her slow and careful, then turned to go out the open front door. That's when he saw me, and I stared him in the eye, letting him know that he better not try any of his loving-dad bullshit on me, else I'd bash his fucking skull in.

When all that was left of him was the sound of his truck rattling away, Sandy walked over and hugged me. "Oh, baby, I'm sorry," she said. "I'm so sorry for what we done to you."

At Bobbie's the next day things were getting pretty heavy on her couch, and I thought she was ready, so I started tugging at the elastic of her panties. It was killing me how worked up I was. But she grabbed my hand and pulled it up to her face and kissed it, then set it on her throat.

"Do you want to choke me?" she asked. "Lizard used to like doing that."

Bobbie talked about him like he was the coolest thing ever. Tattoos, pierced tongue, stupid fucking nickname—he had it all apparently.

"You can, if you want to," Bobbie was saying in a breathy voice meant to be sexy.

And so I did, soft at first, not wanting to hurt her. She started rubbing my legs and crotch, giving me a seductive look, so I squeezed harder, and she rubbed harder, like she was getting into it, and I wondered if she was thinking about Lizard and if maybe this meant she was ready and this was only the beginning, so I pressed down and squeezed and got my other hand over her throat and squeezed. Her face was going red, but she kept rubbing on me so I kept squeezing harder, and I could feel the bendy tube of her throat giving way under my fingers, until finally she slapped at my arms and I let go.

"Are you okay?"

"Yeah, that was fun, don't you think?"

"Do you want to do it?"

"Not tonight," she said and grabbed my shirt and pulled me to her and kissed me. "But we will."

We lay there for a long time, holding each other, and then we watched some TV until just before when her mom was supposed to get home, and I left. She didn't tell me to go, but

I didn't want to be there when her mom got back. The room felt weird just thinking of her mom being there.

It was a few days later that Dean started packing his things. He was visiting a friend in South Carolina he told Sandy, just going hunting for a few days. I was on the couch, eating chips and flipping the channels. I was supposed to meet Bobbie in a little while, and she'd hinted that maybe tonight was the night. Her mom had just gotten her prescription refilled and would be at work until late in the a.m., so we had a little private time planned. I had stolen a Lifestyle Extra Thin from Dean's underwear drawer and already had it in my pocket along with what little was left of my weed. Bobbie and I had smoked almost all of it, but between her mom's valium and this, we would be plenty fucked up. And I didn't want to get too wasted, since I'd heard that sometimes makes your dick not work, and I didn't want anything to go wrong.

"Don't lie to me," Sandy was saying. "What's going on?"

"Nothing. Just a little vacation."

"A little vacation."

I turned the TV off and got up to go.

"You guys are both such douchebags," I said real quiet, not even angry. I didn't like seeing Sandy acting that way and crying. It made me mad at Dean but at her too for some reason.

As I opened the screen door, I looked back at Dean shoving his stupid stuff into a ratty duffle bag and Sandy waving her arms at him and stomping all around. I could still hear her voice pleading when I jumped on my skateboard and pushed off hard three, four times and glided toward Bobbie's sky-blue trailer down at the other end of Whispering Grove. I gave the Lifestyle in my pocket a little pat, just to make sure it was really there, and let the excitement of the evening ahead take over all my thoughts.

THE GOOD EARTH, THE MUD

I got out to Jess's place late on a Friday evening. It was early November and the sky was uncluttered by clouds. It was so sweet and calm with the cool air and the fanning maple leaves—it made me realize how long it'd been since I'd gotten out of the city. Becca had left him again. He told me it might be for good this time. I asked him what had happened, but he wouldn't say, not on the phone. "Bring your shotgun," he said, "we'll get drunk and take the dogs out and see what we can shoot."

I told Jess I had business to take care of—I was working at the time as a day laborer down on I-77 where they were putting in two extra lanes "to accommodate the economic and cultural growth of Charlotte, the Queen City"—but that I could come late the next week, or maybe the one following.

It was three weeks later I got another call from him, and when I recognized his voice, I was hit with a shot of guilt.

"How you been?" I asked.

"You know . . . about as well as can be expected."

"Man, I'm glad you called," I lied. "Is the invite to come out there and break some shit still open?"

"If you're interested."

"Hell yes I'm interested. These guys on the construction job I was telling you about have been working my skinny ass to the bone."

We made plans and I canceled a date I had with a pretty girl named Anne, which was too bad but probably would end up working in my favor in the long run. She was a bartender and what they call a nontraditional student at UNC-Charlotte, because she was in her mid-twenties, just a few years younger than me. And she was serious as hell about her name. "Anne with an *e*," she always said. I get a kick out of people who are so serious about their names. Me, I don't give a flying flipping Fig Newton fuck about my name. Call me asshole or Jesus, I'm still me.

As I drove down the long gravel driveway to his trailer, I wondered what state he'd be in.

I didn't see him at first. I walked up to the screen door, and as I was about to open it, I noticed his stooped form shadowed in the gauzy metal screen. Jess is a tall man, long-shanked and skinny, wiry with muscle. Seeing him standing there like that, like he'd been waiting since day-one of the goddamned universe, made me wish I'd come running the minute he called. He opened the door like a movie character, like Igor or the Hunchback of motherfucking Notre Dame.

"Welcome to my humble abode," he said, emphasizing the word *abode*. Jess had dropped out of high school the minute he was legally allowed, which is sixteen in the State of North Carolina, but he sometimes took to a fancy word and relished it the way a dog will a rawhide bone, chewing on it and coming back to it over and over. He waved me into the messy trailer with a bow and a big wave of his hand and a toothy grin. Becca had been gone only a month, but the trailer already smelled like he'd been living alone for a year or more, and beer bottles rested empty on every flat surface.

"Mind if I open a window?"

"Help yourself. My abode is yours," he said. "Here, catch."

I sat near the window, opening my beer, and thinking how this was going to be a rough weekend. The week had been a tiring one, working outside, being new guy on the crew, and not even permanent, though I hoped they'd take me on full-time after I showed them what kind of worker I was. I sank into Jess's couch and steeled myself for what I was going to have to do. As long as I'd known Jess, he was the emotional type—apt to tell someone he loved them or scream at a stranger or get into a fight when some man flirted with Becca or just sit in a bar and drink all night, staring at the dark tabletop like it held the only truth there was in this shit world.

I didn't think Becca was serious about this break-up. They must've broken up a dozen times or more in the three years they were married, your classic strobe-light relationship. People always thought she'd go for a guy with a bit more brains, a bit more of a future than Jess, but they never could get each other out of their blood. Back when they were still just dating, it was the same. I'm not proud of it, but during one of their early break-ups, Becca and I were drunk and ended up in the sack. I wish I hadn't done it, but she was a looker and was a lot of fun to joke around with. She could have a good laugh with you. She had a real sense of humor, you could say. After we got done fucking, she said they ought to put different warnings on beer.

"Everyone knows it's bad for you," she said, "but what they ought to warn you about it is that it'll make you say the damnedest things to people and have sex with people you shouldn't."

I scooted myself up against her and started rubbing her back. "Yeah, but the best sex is sex you shouldn't be having," I said. She laughed and we were right back at it.

When Jess found out, he told me it was okay, that we'd been friends too long to let it get in the way, but I could tell he wanted to gut me like a fish. I said I was sorry about a thousand times, that it was an accident, and so forth—all the stupid shit you say in that situation—until finally he told me to shut up and never talk about it again.

"Check this out," Jess was saying now. "I just learned how to do this from Chuck, the bartender down at Sally's." He opened a bottle of Pabst and tossed the cap on the counter but didn't watch as it bounced to the kitchen floor. There were about fifty caps scattered all over. "You know how you can shotgun a can of beer but can't a bottle, right?" He was speaking fast and his hands were shaking. I nodded. "Well, Chuck showed me how you can shotgun a bottle." He grabbed a straw, one of the bendy ones you give kids, and put it into the bottle. He waved his hand at the straw sticking out of the bottleneck, like he was demonstrating something important, like he was about to perform magic. Then he bent the straw down, onto the side of the bottle, and showed me, slowly, how to hold it down.

"Okay, now watch." Tilting back, he guzzled the whole thing faster than seemed possible.

"*Jesus*," I said.

"Yeah, no shit, right? Something about air pressure or a vacuum," he said. "I don't know. Chuck showed it to me."

The rest of the night went more or less like that. I told him about Anne, and how she had tits better than the airbrushed ones in Playboy. She had dropped out of college a couple of times, even though her parents were paying for it, which is why we met at Second Place, a bar and grill we both worked at until I quit—me in the kitchen, her in the bar where those tits brought her in three, four hundred dollars a night in tips from guys she mostly didn't want anything to do with. But her parents had gotten tired of paying for school, so now she had to do it herself. "That's so Anne," I told him. "She wouldn't go to school when her parents told her to, but soon as she had to do it on her own, she went and was getting all A's in her classes." I thought I might call Anne, if Jess and I didn't stay up all night drinking.

As I was telling him about her, I realized talking about dating this great girl probably was not the best way to cheer Jess up. For some reason I always do that, always talk until I've said the thing I really ought not to say, but there I am saying it. But instead of shutting up like I should have, I kept going. I told him I had two more classes at the community college and I'd have my welding certification. Then I could make some real money. Twenty-five, thirty bucks an hour, and all the work a man could ask for. And after a couple of years, I planned to open my own welding company. I told Jess maybe we could go in together and be partners. He could move down to Charlotte. "Just think, man, all the young pussy you can handle and money coming in by the fistful. Just think of it. We'll be the kings of the Queen City." That was something a guy on the construction crew said a lot, about the kings and all, and I liked the way it sounded when he said it, but it sounded stupid when I heard myself.

"That's fine and good for you," Jess said. "But I'd just hold you back. I fuck up just about everything."

"Don't talk like that," I said. "You shouldn't talk like that."

"You want me to lie, then? That what you want?"

"I want you to talk like the Jess I know, the ornery fucker too stupid to know when he's beat." Jess and I used to talk to each other that way, insulting ourselves or each other to rile us up. Sometimes insults are the only way to make a person feel good about themselves again.

"I guess I wised up some," he said.

"Oh, come on," I said. "You can get any pretty girl you want, so long as you know the trick."

Jess looked at me, then took a big drink of his beer.

"You just have to ignore pretty girls," I said. "They're so used to guys ogling them, what you have to do is not pay them any attention. They go bat-shit crazy. They can't handle it. And soon enough, they're begging." I got up to get another beer. "That's all, man. You just have to know the trick."

On my way back, I saw a pistol on the kitchen table, mostly hidden by clutter of the KFC and Burger King variety. I picked it up and looked it over. Jess had the best guns. He was always going to gun shows, looking for a deal. This one here was probably one of his little finds. It was a nickel-plated job with faux-wood grip. I didn't know the makes of guns the way Jess did, but I knew a good gun when I saw one.

"Sweet piece," I said and sighted the wall on the other side of the living room. It had a nice weight to it.

"It's a Beretta 84 Cheetah," he said. "I got the thirteen-round clip for no extra. And that's real wood."

I looked again at the handle. The finish on it made it feel

fake, but I guess it was real. Jess knew his shit. And I was glad to hear him talk about it, because he sounded happy talking about the pistol, or not happy, but at least like he was alive again.

The sky was turning gray-blue, and I thought how serious hunters were just now getting up to go out into the woods. But, then, Jess and I never claimed to be serious hunters. It was probably around five a.m. that I finally asked him if he had anything to eat in the house. I still hadn't asked him what he'd done to make Becca leave, not wanting to talk about it really, and I stupidly hoped we just wouldn't get around to talking about it. We finished another beer while he cooked sausage and eggs and threw some dried-out cornbread in a pan with about half a stick of butter to moisten it. We ate using our hands.

"Becca took the silverware with her," Jess said. That was the first time I thought she really might be gone for good.

Lying on the couch, I could hear Jess snoring in the other room, louder than I would have thought a person could snore. *No wonder she left the sonuvabitch*, I thought. My body was worn-out but I couldn't sleep. I lay there for a while thinking about Anne back in Charlotte. She'd read me some Russian lady's poems before I left to come out to Jess's. In one poem, the woman said she was happy that the man she was talking to and her didn't need each other, didn't share a sickness, because when he left she didn't care. After she read that to me, I couldn't think of love without thinking of it as a sickness we give or catch.

I had to piss, so I got up to go outside. On my way out, I saw the Cheetah sitting on the table and grabbed it. I stood on the porch, naked and pissing. I aimed the pistol at my car, a beat up Saturn, and then aimed it at the moon. It was too cold to be standing out there like that, but it felt good, with no one for miles to see the idiot things I was doing. That was what I missed about living in the country—the freedom to do any damn thing that came into your head. I walked out onto the yard in my bare feet and felt the good earth, the mud, beneath me.

Around three o'clock in the afternoon, after we woke up and ate, we were bouncing our way up an old logging path, two dirt rivets with a thin spine of green curving through the middle. Jess's truck rattled as if to come apart. Yellow and brown leaves were matted to the ground. Late afternoon sun was cutting through tall, bare trees—black gum and maple and elm. In Charlotte, where they're developing the suburbs so fast, you see deer running around in people's backyards because the year before it had been forest. And the deer are too stupid to take a different path than they're used to. It's weird and sad to see them running around with the eight-lane roads and malls and nice condos for the upwardly mobile bastards.

"Weather's no good for hunting," Jess said. "Too wet and too sunny."

I didn't know why wet and sunny made for bad hunting. I never much cared for hunting, to tell the truth. When I was a boy, I used to think about hunting the hunters instead of the animals. The way I saw it, the animals needed more help than the hunters did, so I should be on their team. I never killed anything, because I never really aimed. But I was the best at shooting bottles or cans or whatever other junk we set up for target practice. I've always thought I could kill a person sooner than I could kill an animal.

"Then we'll shoot cans or whatever we can find, like when we were kids," I said.

He kept his eyes on the road and I looked out the window at the trees and the underbrush. I was already looking forward to being back in Charlotte.

"Hey, did I tell you about Anne reading me poetry?"

"No," Jess said. "You also didn't tell me you were gay."

"Fuck off. No, seriously. She read this one to me about how love is a sickness, and I thought you might like that idea."

"Why the hell would I like that?"

"I don't know. I just thought you might."

"You knew Becca," Jess said. "You know her recreant ways."

Here it goes, I thought, hoping he wouldn't keep using his word-a-day vocabulary on me.

"Do you think she's coming back?" he asked.

"There's no way to tell what she's going to do. You'd know better than me."

"She's living in Gastonia. She's living with some man named Vincent. What kind of name is that anyway?"

"You know how she is," I said. "She'll be back."

"I know she thought she deserved better than me."

"That's not true," I said.

"I don't think she's coming back."

"If she does, she does. If she doesn't, to hell with her."

"You haven't changed a bit," Jess said and laughed a little.

Jess pulled the truck into a clearing littered with the trash an old campsite. This was one of the spots people came to party. I was surprised to see that the spot hadn't changed since I'd left Shelby County. I guess I shouldn't have been, since not much else had changed either.

We opened beers and used Chuck's shotgun method to empty them. I set our two empties up on the trunk of an overturned cedar, along with a few other bottles and cans I found lying on the ground.

"Let me shoot that," I said.

I missed the first two shots. It'd been a long time since I'd shot a pistol. But the third one hit and so did the fourth. Jess was shotgunning another beer, so I fired the rest of the clip, leaving one can untouched.

"Not bad for a Charlotte boy," Jess said.

"Let's see how you do."

I walked around and found more targets and set them up. When I turned around, Jess had the Cheetah raised and aimed right at me. We stood there looking at each other.

"Well," he said. "Get out of my way. Or do I have to shoot you first?"

I walked back to where Jess was standing. I grabbed a beer. Jess raised the pistol and emptied the clip so fast he only hit one of the bottles. He reloaded quicker than I thought possible, and then emptied the clip again just as fast. This time he got two more. He began reloading again and dropped a few bullets on the ground.

"Hey, Bull's-eye, give me a shot at it," I said.

I saw that he was crying. I hate it when people cry. I have no idea what to do around people who are crying.

"What's the worst way to die?"

"What the hell are you talking about? Don't be stupid." I held my hand out for him to give me my turn with the gun.

Jess put the Beretta to the side of his head. "What if I just blew my brains out? How would she like that, do you think?" He pressed the barrel harder against his temple until the skin went dead white.

"Stop fooling around."

"I'm not fooling. What else am I supposed to do?"

He's going to do it, I thought. My face went numb and sweat rose up all over my skin and an empty place like falling opened in the pit of my stomach. My knees were rubbery, and I told myself not to piss my pants. It was like they always say on television about how time slows down. Every one of my thoughts came to me slow and clear, but I couldn't move. I worried about what would happen if he did it. Would the police think I'd killed him? My fingerprints were all over the pistol. But I could explain that. The bottles. Maybe I could explain it. At least he wasn't going to shoot me. But how would I get back to tell them about it? I'd have to get his keys from his pocket to drive back into town. It might look like I stole his truck. I could just walk. Why did my fingerprints have to be on the goddamned pistol?

"Please don't do this. I'm sorry, Jess. You're better than her. I—don't, just don't, please, please."

He looked up into the canopy of trees and the muscles in his neck tensed. I closed my eyes and thought again not to piss myself.

"I can't," he said.

I opened my eyes as he was handing me the pistol. I took the clip out and slid it into my back pocket and put the pistol in my jacket pocket, not for any good reason, but just to be doing something.

"I can't even do this," he said.

"That's good, man," I said. "That's a good thing."

He handed me the Cheetah without me even asking for it and just looked at me until I had to look away. I turned my head toward the truck. "Give me the keys. I'll drive us back."

I drove us through the woods, down the long green spine of the logger's trail. Once we got back on the road, and the tires were whirring smoothly with the wet hiss of the rain-covered asphalt below us, I looked over at Jess and almost said something but didn't know what I might say if I opened my mouth, and so I kept it shut. His face was pressed against the window and I thought how cool the moist glass must feel. I knew when we got back to his place, I couldn't just get in my car and leave like I wanted. We would have to find a place to eat dinner, and then we'd probably end up drunk again. By then I'd know the things to say, and how to say them. But as I drove, I only wanted to get back to Charlotte, back to Anne, back to my life. To hell with all this, I thought.

"The weather's changing. It's going to be a prepossessing day" Jess said and laughed a bit as he rolled down the window, letting the wet air blow in on us.

Lonely Tylenol

Red had wasted himself on the pipe all night and was rummaging the fibers of the carpet for little imagined chunks of crack, his fingers fidgeting with hope and need, while a man in the kitchen was telling his brother about a woman so perfect it made his balls clench up just thinking of her. He told his brother that if he could lasso a winged heart like hers, he'd walk a straight path the rest of his life and become the man he was intended to be. He maintained that he was a philosopher first and a poet second, that without the lift of idea, beautiful words were as stupid as daisies growing on unmade graves. His brother grunted agreement, slumped heavily against the sink, eyes wandering in and out, lower lip dripping saliva and beer. He'd heard all this before, knew its majesty and circumstance by heart.

"Lonely Tylenol, lonely Tylenol, lonely Tylenol," a bright-faced boy maybe nine was saying down the hallway for someone who might care. "Forwards and backwards, it spells the same. Lonely Tylenol," he instructed, proud scientist of words, and gave the bottle a little musical shake.

The Kitchen Philosopher was explaining how this woman had made him feel like the Jack of fucking Hearts, like King of the World, and how all he needed to be a happy man was to bring her the slightest pleasure. And he meant that with a lowercase and capital P.

Red's sister, Wanda, came into the living room and was yelling at him to get out of her house, that she didn't want that shit he was on around her and her son, that she'd call the goddamn police if he didn't get out the door right then and there. Red focused on her, fear and sadness on his face, stood, and walked out of the house, muttering expletives and whipped-dog whines on his shuffling way. The door clicked behind him without conviction, and Wanda waited nearly a minute before locking it. Her head shook absently, unbelieving of the blue-gray streaks of paint on the glass of the door where the painters had slopped the job they weren't paid much to do.

"That sonuvabitch," she said, back in the kitchen, pouring a too-strong, bottom-shelf gin and tonic. She gulped at her drink, swearing to never speak to her brother again.

The Kitchen Philosopher stopped talking of his lofty and unattained love, felt sympathy for the crow's feet of Wanda's eyes, the thickness of her waist, her job in Kroger's meat department, the poverty her life had been. He thought he could have loved her once as well. All that unmoored heft.

"Mommy, look. Lonely Tylenol," the boy said. "Do you see?"

"That's great, baby. It's time for bed now. Let mommy and her friends be."

The boy walked to the far end of the hallway, where his room gaped, glowing yellow from a bedside lamp, a rattle of pills in his hand.

The Kidnapping

I t wasn't a kidnapping at all, or not a real one, not like the ones you see in the movies with abandoned houses and rickety wooden chairs and duct tape. But Tanner's mother insisted on calling it that, and the district attorney insisted on calling it that, and that was the verdict of the judge despite what Tanner tried to say about what had happened that almost perfect day in October.

Tanner was twelve years old then, and his parents had been divorced for three years. He knew his father was what people called a *bad father* and a *bad husband*. He drank, missed school sporting events, even once threw part of a concrete birdbath through the living room window when Tanner's mother had locked him out of the house. That was just before she divorced him. And Tanner understood why she would divorce him. He had been told dozens of times by friends of the family and his grandparents—both his mother's parents and his father's—that his father was *bad for the family*. No one listened to his father's apologies anymore and everyone listened to his mother's complaints. The listening people of the world were all on her side, so Tanner decided to be on his father's. He had never liked school sporting events either and would have missed them if he could. And how often had he wanted to break windows, puncture tires, set the whole ugly world on fire?

So when his father arrived at school to pick him up—standing in front of his car, looking nervous and sad—even though Tanner's mother had told him not to go anywhere with his father and to call her immediately if his father contacted him, Tanner ran to his father and hugged him, made a big show of how much he loved his father, which he did. He looked up and saw the nervousness and sadness replaced with happiness and salvation, or what Tanner assumed the pastor meant when he spoke of the salvation of sinners.

"How you doing, Big Man?"

"Pretty good, I guess. School sucks."

"Don't say that," his father said. "You have to do well in school. Your grades are still good, right?"

"Yeah. I'm doing good. Especially in geography class. Mrs. Phelps is the best teacher, and I like looking at the maps. But everything else is so stupid."

"It can seem that way sometimes, I know, but keep playing like it isn't and just do what you're supposed to."

Tanner was tired of talking about school and was getting worried that his mother had warned the school about his father.

"Where are we going?"

"Anywhere you want to go, Big Man. Anywhere in the whole fucking world."

They drove to a McDonald's for food. Tanner didn't really want to go to McDonald's, though he did like their French fries, and it was the first place he could think to tell his father he wanted to go. As they talked, his father suggested they go get him a map to put up on his bedroom wall. They went to Wal-Mart and looked in the school supplies section and found a nice colored map of the world. Tanner loved it, every little thing about it. His father bought the map and handed him the bag with the map neatly rolled in it. Tanner put it in his book bag so his mother wouldn't know what he had.

It was time to get Tanner home, his father said. As they drove, Tanner asked, "Father, why are you like you are?"

"You know, it's always cracked me up the way you call me that. Other kids call their dads *Dad*, but not you."

"I just like it better. Sounds more important. But I'm kind of strange. All the kids think so, I can tell, and so does Nathan. I hate him."

"Well, I can't say he's my favorite man, but you shouldn't hate anyone. That's how I got to be the way I am."

The sun had set and they drove the rest of the way in the dark listening to news on the radio. When his father still lived at home, Tanner would sit with him and watch the news. It made him feel adult and made him feel closer to his father. Even now, years after the kidnapping, years after the other tragedies, Tanner still remembers those evenings with his father, and this car ride with him, taking in the news of the world.

When they got to the house, the police were already there. His mother had warned the school officials, as Tanner had worried, and they had called the police. They arrested his father as his mother grabbed Tanner and hugged him and kissed him, asked him if he was okay, making a big show of how much she loved him, which she did. Tanner kept saying, "He didn't hurt me. He didn't do anything." But no one listened to him; his mother, as was her art, had all the listeners. The blue and red of the police lights were alternately muted in the porch-light glow that made a semicircle in the front lawn. After the police were gone, Tanner went into his room and hid the map under his bed. He didn't tell his mother about the map and enjoyed not telling her.

Later that night, Tanner overheard his mother talking with Nathan.

"This is going to ruin his life," Nathan said. "He might even go to jail."

"He should have thought of that."

"He's such a sad case."

"Well, not everyone's life is meant to be happy."

Tanner lay in bed thinking of that idea. Are there people meant to be unhappy? Is anyone meant to be happy, or is it always an accident? He rolled over onto his side and breathed the warm smell of his clean sheets and wondered what kind of person he was—meant for happiness or meant for sadness. Then he decided it was a stupid question since there was no answer. He closed his eyes and named country names until he went to sleep, the whole while imagining that his father could hear him naming the countries, so he picked ones he thought his father would like best. *Uruguay, Brazil, Holland, Italy . . .*

The Names of Distant Galaxies

I still had a couple hours before the wedding, and everyone was too busy fussing over details I either didn't understand or didn't care about, so I threw gravel from the church parking lot at a snake hole I'd found beside the graveyard. It was an early September afternoon and hot. Underneath the tuxedo, I was sweating in the armpits and a little down the back. But there was a breeze I barely noticed, like it was caused by the fanning maple leaves instead of the other way around. The air carried a cool hint of October or November, so I was thinking about pumpkin pie and cranberry sauce as I let the soft bulb of my thumb slide over each piece of gravel, feeling for shape and weight before throwing. I was getting better, and more gravel was going in the hole. I imagined that when the snake woke up, he'd be stuck under a pile of gravel and not be able to get out, or he'd come back and be blocked from his home and get rained on. All of which was more interesting than Shawn's wedding. (After my mother died of her cancer, I began calling my father by his first name. It just felt right, like I had become an adult, or our relationship had changed now that my mother was dead.) I was throwing the gravel pieces left-handed, a challenge I enjoyed, when a hand gripped my arm.

"That tux cost money, you know," Shawn said. "Just look at yourself."

An empty place like falling opened up in my stomach, and I dropped my handful of gravel, stupidly acting innocent. I felt bad for dirtying the tuxedo. I knew it was just gravel dust we could brush off, but I was embarrassed I'd forgotten what everyone must have told me twice about being careful with the expensive rental.

"I'm sorry," I said. "I'll clean it off."

Shawn pulled me to my feet and, still holding onto my arm, smacked my thighs and the seat of my pants harder than needed to get the dust off. It didn't hurt, but I felt bad that he was angry. My father was never a big man, but his wiry muscles and his deep voice made him more intimidating than either his size or his overall gentleness should have allowed. (There has always been something in him that was sturdy and tireless, and this was the first time, as best I can remember, that I'd seen that sturdy quality shift to stern.)

On our way back to the church, I watched his heels lift and set, as I tried to keep up. My chest and face were tingling. As we walked up the five steps to the entrance I noticed the paint around the door was peeling back, revealing grayed wood underneath. I remembered that Jeremy, Shawn's best man, kept saying this was the most important day in Shawn's life, then patting him on the shoulder. And though I knew, even as young as I was, that I should be more mature, I couldn't help but want everything to go wrong.

2

I am shocked by how many details of the wedding I remember. But also by the many I don't. I should call Shawn tomorrow and ask him about that day—it's been months since we've talked, so I really should call anyway. It'll be easy enough; I can just say I was feeling nostalgic, since I am about to be married myself. There are other things I remember, especially later that night after the wedding, that I shouldn't mention to him, but we can have a safe-enough conversation, I'd think.

Enough writing for today. I'm not sure if I'll continue it, even though Simone tells me I should. It does nothing for my real research, and I don't have time to waste, since I am up for tenure review next year. But there is something enjoyable about the process of writing down my memories, like I'm getting to know myself in a way. It's also fun to play at being a writer.

3

I looked at the pillow in my hands and the little plastic rings tied on it for decoration. They didn't trust me with the real ones. I was too young they said. I focused on the pillow and the fake rings—those two little yellow circles and their pink bows—and I thought about what the preacher was saying until it was time for Shawn and Flora to put on the real rings and kiss.

I tried not to stare at Flora. Shawn had told me about how, because of her disease, *dystonia* it was called, she couldn't control her muscles, and that's why she moved like that all the time. I'd heard the word dozens of times—*dystonia*—a beautiful word reminiscent of foreign countries, the scientific names for flowers, and distant galaxies. Odd that such a word could mean *crippling disease*. I also always thought of diseases like these happening to people in New York City or California or Japan, not in rural Kentucky.

When the time came, Shawn nodded at me, which was annoying, since I knew it was time for my part in the performance. I stepped up between them, like we'd practiced several times the day before, and they acted like they were taking the rings from the pillow even though they already had them. And though I knew I wasn't actually doing anything, I mimicked the gravity of the preacher's tone and words, and for a moment, I felt it too.

Shawn got Flora's ring over her cramping finger, but she

fumbled with his, nearly dropping it twice. Shawn finally put it on himself, smiling, and the preacher said that he may now kiss the bride. Flora's lips smeared over his as her head moved back and forth in quick diagonal jerks. They finished and everyone clapped. Flora blushed a little. Shawn continued smiling and straightened his back like he'd won the biggest prize he could think of. I don't remember much else from the ceremony. It was a small church. I felt important standing in front of so many people. I liked the way everyone's attention electrified the air around us. But I didn't forget how wrong it was that my father was marrying this woman.

There were a few cousins and old high school friends on the groom's side, nothing much to speak of. My cousin Kyle wore jeans and an Ohio State Buckeyes football tie, partly as a joke and partly because he loved his football. He'd driven most of the groom's guests down from Columbus. Flora had dozens of aunts, uncles, cousins, and an assortment of friends, several of which were variously afflicted with crippling diseases, friends from Flora's past, when she still attended support groups. Photographers—who had been instructed to catch Flora with her mouth closed and head turned forward—fretted over every shot. They seemed to enjoy the challenge, and Harold had promised them a good tip if the photos came out to Flora's liking.

The limousine ride to the reception was nice. Jenny, who'd been the flower girl in the wedding, rode with us. I wanted to stick my head out of the sunroof the way they do in movies, but I didn't think that would be proper. Especially after I'd already messed up once that day. Also, I'd decided to be quiet and angry.

The reception was in Liberty, twenty-five miles away, and the driver took a long, scenic route to make sure we got our money's worth. I looked out the window, imagining myself as Iron Man, from the comics I read, flying alongside the limousine. I smashed trees with my armored fists, fired repulsor beams at buildings and enjoyed the spray of debris. I weaved between telephone poles and tree branches. When that got boring, I grabbed the telephone wires and rocketed upward, tearing poles from the ground, then flung them miles away. I thought about how Tony Stark, Iron Man's secret identity, was a genius who could solve any problem in his labs.

I remembered the years Shawn and I had spent living together, just the two of us. I wanted to ask how Shawn could allow this one day to outweigh those years, allow it to outweigh the nights of us cooking frozen pizzas together, of us figuring out how to be a family without my mother there. We were more like roommates or best friends than father and son. And now I felt all of that being erased.

By the time we got to the reception, the other guests had arrived and already started in on the food and the champagne fountain. I had never been around so many adults talking before. Everyone was flirting the way people will after a wedding. Old women were walking up to Shawn's now father-in-law, Harold, and calling him a crazy old man or dirty geezer and then poking him in the ribs when his wife, Fern, wasn't looking. Younger unmarried men were asking women how far up they thought Flora had put the garter and if they should try to catch it.

I stood against a wall and sulked, hoping Shawn would come and ask me what was wrong, but he was consumed in all the hubbub. There was music playing so I went to the dance floor, because I had nothing else to do, and I was getting bored with my hurt-son act. I liked the way the rented shoes slid around as I moved, and the tuxedo made me feel I could dance better than usual. Jeremy and another of Shawn's friends, Ray, were dancing with Teresa and Carrie Blake, the girls who ran California Flicks, the sole video store in Liberty, Kentucky. Their father, one of the richest men in the area, owned the store and had handed over management to them after they'd graduated high school one year apart but showed no interest in going to college. Everyone talked about how pretty they were, and they knew it. Jeremy and Ray were having a great time, making asses of themselves and trying to be funny, creating a spectacle of being with such pretty girls.

After a while Carrie squatted down and, shortened to my level, danced with me. She was just trying to amuse the others, which I think I might have realized even then, but that didn't stop the skin on my face from tingling with excitement. I had thought she was beautiful since the first time Shawn and I visited Liberty, back when Shawn and Flora began dating about a year earlier. And Carrie was always nice to me.

I loved dancing, and because I loved doing it so much, I guess I was pretty good at it.

"Look at this boy!" Carrie said, laughing and looking back at the others. "He can really move his rump."

"Hell yeah, Andrew, shake that thing!" Jeremy yelled. But he wasn't going to let himself be outdone; he ran over to where Jenny was standing on the edge of the dance floor, trying to build her courage to join in, and dragged her to the center of our small group. By now everyone in the room was watching them. Jenny was giggling as Jeremy swung her and twirled her around. The corners of Carrie's lips were stretching toward her rounded cheekbones. I wanted to kiss her right on the mouth and run away.

Then it came time for Shawn and Flora to open their presents. [*This part is a bit of a blur in my memory, since I didn't really care about most of the gifts, but certain items stick out. They lifted crock-pots and gag gifts alike to show the circle of friends and family members gathered. The crowd ooh-ed at the expensive ones, ha-ha-ed at the silly ones, made conspiratorial remarks about those designed for bedroom use. The issue will be to get this into the way I thought about it then, which I really don't remember. I was probably halfway fascinated and halfway bored out of my mind.*]

When all the wrapping paper was torn away and the gifts set aside for later inventory, someone yelled for Flora to throw her bouquet. The DJ said over the loudspeakers that all the young ladies should come up front and try their luck. Reluctantly or theatrically, each of them joined the wall of women between Flora and the non-participants: men young or old and women who had traded their right to catch for the one-time chance to throw.

Flora turned her back to them and threw the bouquet over her shoulder, straining to throw it hard enough and straight. It flew high and at an awkward angle, but Carrie took a few quick steps, stretched her arm, caught it with the tips of two fingers. She faced the other women who hadn't moved and bowed like a concert pianist. A few came to inspect the bouquet like botanists or clairvoyants trying to figure what it meant.

Flora beamed at how well everything was turning out.

The DJ started playing a slow cabaret song and in a sulky baritone told the boys the time they'd been waiting for was here. Jeremy pushed Shawn toward Flora. Shawn looked at everyone like he was saying it was all Jeremy's fault, laughing and pretending to struggle against him. He threw up his arms in mock defeat and walked the rest of the way on his own. He knelt down in front of her and lifted her dress so that her left knee showed. When at first he didn't see the garter he asked if it was on the other leg. She made an exaggerated shake of her head saying no, her jaw stretching open uncontrollably and twin globules of spittle forming in the corners of her mouth. Shawn pushed the dress up even further. Half of her thigh was uncovered by the time we saw the garter. Andrew heard several hoots of approval and leaned to get a better view like several people around him. Her deeply browned leg was thin and tense like a swimmer's.

I felt that I shouldn't be looking at her leg because she was going to be my mother now more or less, and because of her disease, but I kept looking. Her leg looked normal, attractive even. Before, she had always seemed freakish or alien. Now she seemed human with everyone laughing and her laughing too. Shawn stood up and spun the garter around his forefinger before sending it sailing into the air at the men lined up as if before a firing squad. I was confused when Jeremy jumped in front of the others and snatched the garter mid-flight. Catching meant, according to everything I had heard, that Jeremy would be the next man married, and he must have said a hundred times in the past week that he was never getting married.

Jeremy trotted toward Carrie, brandishing the garter like a dagger at the other men, as though they were cartoon lions and he a valiant gladiator.

"Looks like we're next," he said.

After Shawn, Flora, Jeremy, and Carrie had danced the traditional slow dances, and the photographs were taken, the reception thinned rapidly. Shawn asked Jeremy if he'd watch after me. Jeremy winked with meaning I was beginning to understand and said it wouldn't be any trouble. He laid his arms across my shoulders and hugged me, but I squirmed from his grasp.

"Why can't I stay with you and Flora?" I asked.

"After their wedding, a man and wife want to be together. We'll all have a big breakfast tomorrow morning. You stay with Jeremy tonight. And mind him, you hear?"

When we'd lived in Columbus, I'd spent plenty of nights at Jeremy's place while Shawn was at work. Jeremy was like an older brother to me, or an uncle, part of our hodgepodge family. I watched Shawn walk to where Flora was sitting surrounded by a semi-circle of women, each one leaning in and talking in high-pitched voices.

"Andrew, you listening?" Jeremy asked.

"Yeah. What did you say?"

"I said me and you'll ride with Ray," he said and ruffled my hair. "Let's get going. We have a long ride ahead of us."

It was dark now, and the reception hall, which doubled as a performance hall for church choirs and school bands, looked square and squat under the dull, yellow light of the streetlamps. I looked out the window as the dusk-lit city receded and the open stretch of the interstate snaked out before us.

"What d'you picture the honeymoon'll look like?" Ray said and forced a mischievous giggle. "I don't know if I could handle her moving around under me like that." Ray shook his head and clucked his disbelief at the world. "I'd have to close my eyes. Or tie her down maybe."

"Shut up, Ray," Jeremy said and motioned toward me in the backseat.

"Oh, I didn't mean anything by it," Ray said. "Andrew, did I offend you any?"

I didn't know. Was I offended? I didn't think so, but Jeremy kept glaring straight ahead, his jaw muscles tensing like he was chewing a bag of rusty nails.

"Just be quiet, Ray."

They drove the rest of the way in silence except for Ray fiddling with the radio. The night skimmed by outside the window, and gooseflesh rose up on my arms and neck. The headlights cut bright wounds that healed themselves with dark oily ointment, leaving only the brief redness of the taillights as proof of our passage.

It wasn't until we stepped out of the car and started toward Jeremy's apartment that I noticed Teresa and Carrie sitting on the hood of their car drinking beer from cans. Ray gave a high-pitched holler. Jeremy smiled and led the way to his apartment. Carrie hopped off the car athletically and caught up with him. Teresa eased herself down, careful not to get beer on her skirt, and toasted with Ray to weddings and free alcohol. I followed a few feet behind them. All I wanted was sleep.

4

This is probably not usable for the novel or memoir or whatever this is (the Word file is titled novel_memoir_thingie.doc), but I remember that night more vividly than most in my childhood, and for no obvious reason. I lay in bed listening to the four of them party. I still will be struck with the memory—totally at random, while ordering a coffee or taking a shower—of hearing two voices in the living room, Ray's and one of the girls, and then hearing Jeremy's bedroom door click shut with a noise that was laden with sexual import. I strained to figure out which girl's voice I was hearing in the living room, but I couldn't make it out with the door shut and the air conditioner running. I have no idea why that bothered me so much. Hell, in some small way, it still does today. If

I wouldn't sound insane, I would want to call Jeremy and ask whether it was Carrie or Teresa. I assume it was Carrie. But you never know about these things, I've learned. (For example, I was dating my fiancée's roommate when we first met.)

5

I sat behind the dark orange barn doodling in my notebook. Late-afternoon sunlight warmed the straw scattered loosely about. The white paper reflected a mild yellow around my jagged pencillings. I had drawn three squarish boxes, each picturing a chapter in a story.

In the first box three figures stood in stair-step order, descending left to right. The tallest one wore a baseball cap on his circular head and held a line-thin pitchfork with a hand attached to an equally thin arm; his belt buckle was larger than its smiling face. The middle figure wore a gray dress adorned with gray daisies; her gray, stringy hair partially covered her calm, gray face; there were writhing squiggles to either side of each leg and arm. The shortest one frowned as a gray cloud flung raindrops and lightning bolts at his head.

In the second box a sports car and a naked figure with no arms and implausibly large breasts had arrived. The first two figures from the previous caption looked at each other, question marks scribbled above their heads. The rain cloud was now gone.

The final panel depicted two confused figures crying as a sports car raced off, leaving a puff of indifferent dust behind. The word *VROOM* floated mid-air like a flock of gray birds.

I heard a car coming up the driveway, which meant Shawn was home from work. I closed my notebook and ran to the house. Flora was in the kitchen cutting potatoes and carrots for the beef stew she was making.

"Shawn's home."

"Well, go get him a beer. I'm busy right now." Then, cutting a potato into quarters—her uncontrolled jaw somewhat garbling the words—"and get yourself a Coke if you want."

She slid the cut pieces into a bowl and started on another potato. Her cramped hands were like fleshy spiders maneuvering the knife and potato. It'd been two months since the wedding, but I still watched closely as she performed complicated tasks, especially if it involved blades or hot pans. Outside, the dirt and rock of the driveway popped and crunched under Shawn's tires. The car stopped in front of the house as I stepped into the laundry room where the refrigerator was. (Because of the way the house was wired that was the only room it could go.) My socks and underclothes were lying unattended on top of the dryer. I opened the refrigerator and grabbed a beer, considered grabbing a second one, wondered whether anyone would even notice, but instead pulled out a can of Dr Chek. The sun was shining at a low angle, reflecting off the Formica counter where I set Shawn's beer. I knew Harold and Fern would be walking the mile or so of dirt road from their house to ours by now. They came for dinner everyday.

Flora didn't argue about the living arrangement and seemed happy to see her father, though her mood was brighter when Fern couldn't make it on Tuesdays, bingo night, when she drove into town with the five dollars she allotted herself to lose. On nights Fern was there, she retraced Flora's steps, making sure enough pepper had been used, not too much butter (Harold's heart was getting old after all), the temperature was correct for casseroles.

"If you ever need any help, you know you can call me."

"I know, Mom," Flora said.

"Does Andrew help out?" Then to me, as though she were my mother, "Andrew, you best help Flora more. I see you all the time out behind the barn playing at your foolishness or scribbling in that notebook of yours."

I looked to where I had set my notebook by the sink and remembered the drawings. I assured Fern that I would help more. I grabbed my notebook as though cleaning up after myself. This pleased her, and she patted me on the back as I passed them on the way to my room.

"That boy's in the clouds. He never had proper upbringing," she said. "A boy needs a mother to teach him how to act."

"Andrew's a fine boy. Leave him alone."

I felt spite and pride—but mostly spite—that Flora had defended me. Outside I could hear Shawn and Harold talking. I strained to distinguish what they were saying, Harold more than Shawn, because I liked listening to him talk. Each word rolled off Harold's tongue like a small stone smoothed and wetted by his old-man's Kentucky accent, like it'd been left in a swift-flowing creek for a casual century. I used to just listen to the noises of his words sometimes, ignoring their meaning entirely. For the most part I disliked the overbearing rural accent of the young and middle-aged in the area, but a man of sixty or seventy could carry the lilts and dips naturally, working a certain rough magic.

They walked by my bedroom window on their way inside but didn't see me watching them. Their faces were solemn and tense. I strained harder but still couldn't hear what they were saying. In the kitchen I heard Fern talking again.

"I can't believe Harold is giving in to Gary, no matter how much money he's offering."

Not wanting to miss anything, I went into the kitchen and started grabbing silverware and plates to set the table, hoping that by proving helpful I would earn the right to listen in. Shawn and Harold usually sat at the dinner table to discuss business matters—Shawn with a beer, Harold drinking hot black tea with honey—while Flora and Fern prepared dinner. It was my habit on such occasions to set the table, so I could go back and forth between the kitchen and dining room, eavesdropping on both conversations, but never adding my own input unless the discussion revolved around Christmas, my birthday, vacation trips, or how well I was doing in school. I found the conversations I didn't participate in much more engaging. Listening spy-like—grasping certain parts, being lost by certain others as though they were spoken in a code I had to decipher—gave me the purest, most curious pleasure I knew at that time in my life.

"If I were a monkey, I'd shit in my hand and throw it at him, and you know that well as I do," Harold said. "But Fern and me need the money, with me retired now."

"But there are other ways," Shawn said. "Frank Simmons has been wantin to buy a few acres from you to give his son and daughter-in-law for a house. Why don't you sell him some land? Anything's better than givin in to that sonuvabitch Gary Otis."

Shawn's speech had changed since we'd moved to the farm. It had started when we first started visiting, about a year ago, but the change was bigger when once we moved here for good. He dropped g's from the ends of words (gerunds Mrs. Phelps, my seventh-grade teacher, called them), slurred words together that were never meant to share one breath, and turned perfectly good words into ugly creatures: "wash" became the slug-like "warsh" in his mouth.

"Done and done. Already sold off five acres to Frank last week. He gave me more than a penny for them too, out of the kindness of his heart, more than they're worth." Harold looked into the tea in his cup as he swirled it. "No other choice. I've got to let that numb-nuts Otis build his curing barn here. And then next spring he'll be planting three acres more tobacco, courtesy of Harold Griffin."

"At least tell me you're makin him bleed for it."

"Six fifty now and ten percent of the crop every year."

Shawn considered this, squeezing his eyes half-shut and tilting his head slightly in calculation. He'd been learning about tobacco rates and land value by talking to the men who gathered at Gray's Convenient Store on Saturdays. He relaxed his face into a grin.

"You dirty dog, Harold," he said. "That ain't half bad, not half bad at all."

"Thank you kindly. I do try."

Hearing the discussion was over, Flora walked in to refill Harold's tea and to give Shawn another beer. I followed her back into the kitchen to see what they had made of everything. Fern was smoking a hand-rolled cigarette thin as a pencil lead. (When her doctor told her to quit, she started rolling them thinner and more often). She barely suppressed her smile. She'd decided to dislike any dealings with Gary Otis, and though she was obviously pleased to hear about the success of the transaction, she refused to show it this soon. She would slowly change her demeanor, until eventually she would be completely for it and pretend she had never been against the idea in the first place—"Only a fool would be," she'd say and shrug her shoulders.

During dinner Harold and Shawn mostly repeated how well Harold had done, and damn that old Gary Otis, the bastard best give them their money next month, right after he starts taking his tobacco in for sale. I ate two bowls of beef stew, three pieces of cornbread, a small mountain of hominy, and an equally sized pile of buttered peas. I gulped my milk so noisily Fern smacked my wrist with her napkin to remind me of table manners, but she did it mechanically, not really feeling the spirit to reprimand.

After dinner was done Shawn and Harold went to the tractor barn to work on a tilling blade that'd come loose. As usual I followed them to avoid washing dishes and to learn how to fix things, the true measure of a man's worth in a farming community. It had taken less than a week for me to grow tired of the nickname City Kid. I had not yet accepted farm life into my heart, but I was determined not to be beaten by it. Harold already trusted me to change spark plugs, oil, and air filters on any of the farm vehicles. Shawn sometimes watched me do the work Harold delegated to me, partially to be certain it was done correctly, mostly out of pride. Forcing my involuntary smile to a flat line, I would keep to the task at hand and pretend not to notice him watching me.

But that evening there wasn't anything for me to do but watch Shawn and Harold, so I opened my notebook and tried to draw a barn. While Shawn worked on the tiller, Harold sat on a bucket turned upside down and smoked his pipe, chewing on the end of it between tokes, standing periodically with a puff of yellow-gray smoke to correct some mechanic's error Shawn had made. Shawn finished with the tiller and needlessly cleaned the tractor's engine. I felt I should stay entirely quiet; as if my being there validated them somehow, because without an audience their masculine prowess would go unnoticed, but my voice would have damaged their ritual beyond repair.

My drawing of Gary Otis's barn didn't turn out too well, so I turned to the drawings I had done earlier and felt bad for having drawn them, happy as I was now, just sitting in the loft, my belly full of food, listening to all the evening noises of the farm—insects and wind and the creek in the distance. I tore the drawings out carefully. Then I tore each page over and over until I had a rough confetti and shoved it in my pocket. It felt soft and pillowy, like a cheap stuffed animal or something. I climbed into the upper loft and sat in the hay. The hay-dust went up my nose and I thought I was going to sneeze, but I didn't. I grabbed the pitchfork and turned it in my hands. The points were dull, and I thought how they probably wouldn't even break the skin if you tried to stab someone with them. The handle was worn smooth from use. It was blackened and waxy feeling where Harold's hands had gripped the wood longer than I'd been alive.

6

Should I write about Socrates? I have seen some horrible books about dogs. In fact, I have never seen anything but horrible books about dogs—unless Jack London wrote them maybe.

Simone said, "Write about the dog. You loved that dog."

"Yeah, but what if it sucks?"

"If it sucks, just cut it out."

"I guess."

"Now that you've decided to become a writer or whatever, you're

too serious about all of this stuff. It's your life. Write what matters to you and don't write what doesn't matter to you."

"You're right."

"I know I am," she said in that playfully confident way she has and kissed me. God, I am a lucky son of a bitch.

I guess I should introduce myself, though I have no idea who (if anybody) might read this or in what form. My name is Andrew Wallace and I work in psycholinguistic research at the University of Illinois. My particular field of research is not, as I had assumed it would be, in neurological disorders. I had meant to be a doctor, but I quickly found during an internship I did for Americorps between undergrad and grad school that I have little patience for the human organism and all its endless and endlessly messy vicissitudes. Herpes sores? Blood-saturated shit? Unendurable pain I can do nothing to reduce? No, I am not interested in making these things a part of my daily life, and I know it says something bad about my character that I'm not. But when we follow the philosopher's dictum to know ourselves, where is it written that we should expect to like all of it?

And so, like happens with many starry-eyed youths, I changed my career path when I was confronted with the reality of my dream. Dreams are not made of pretty stuff; just read your Freud and you'll know that. My current work is in the field of psycholinguistics, specifically in trauma—working with rape victims, soldiers back from Iraq suffering from post-traumatic stress disorder, severe car crash survivors, and so on—but my work is almost entirely theoretical. I take case studies and publish articles read by a few specialists in the field, contributing very little to anything except my CV and eventual bid for tenure. My fiancée Simone (about whom I might write more later) tells me I shouldn't belittle my work, that the articles I publish and the so-called pure research or theoretical work I do guides the practical applications others do. Without my work, she tells me, thousands of rape victims or survivors of crippling accidents would not have the resources for recovery they have. She's right in a way. Technically. On paper. In theory, as it were. However you want to phrase it. And I know she's right, though that doesn't change anything.

Why am I writing about my job now? I should write about my dog instead.

7

Socrates pulled against the leash. The muscles in Shawn's arm tensed and separated into sinewy strands. Barking—straining to get to me, the front half of his body suspended off the ground by the choking tension in the leash—Socrates wagged his tail and slobbered joy at my being home. Mrs. Crowley waved goodbye to me once she saw I was safely across the road, and the school bus drove off in a grumbly smell of diesel.

On the days Shawn didn't have to go into Liberty to work, he met me and walked with me back to the house. As the security guard for the Liberty Public Library, he worked odd and irregular hours, leading him to worry, in his Shawn way, that we were not seeing enough of each other, not being enough of a family, so he devised plans to promote familial bonds and happiness—afternoons of lawn games, nights of Monopoly or UNO around the kitchen table, picnics in the farther pastures of the farm.

Wendell Jefferson had advertised at Gray's Convenient Store a one-year old pup he'd like to sell. Shawn bought the pup and brought him home, displaying him with bashful and sincere pride. A small Border collie with a black coat and a white tip of fur on his chin, like a billy goat or a philosopher according to Harold, Socrates was all energy and no direction. Shawn imagined that the added liveliness around the farm would cheer everyone. And I think he'd also hoped the dog would become Flora's personal companion. But Socrates found the little boy I was a much more interesting playmate than any of the adults on the farm. Despite myself, I took to him instantly. I talked to him about my comic books and my theories about science I didn't understand but pretended to, all of which he received with salivating glee. I loved especially that he was named after a great philosopher. I imagined him wise beyond human understanding and asked him questions as we walked through the fields and forest surrounding the house.

[*It seems stupid to say so, but even now, almost twenty years later, I remember them as some of the deepest and most important conversations of my life. I could write something falsely sage like: they were deeper or more important because the questions never got answered. And that would be partially true, but it wasn't the entirety of it. I want to say it wasn't because there were no answers but because I didn't expect answers, so I asked any question I wanted, but I'm not even sure if that makes sense.*]

8

One morning—it must have been a Saturday or a holiday, since I wasn't in school or church—Flora had sat down to a cup of coffee, when I told her I was hungry again.

"You just ate. You can't be hungry again."

I assured her I was. It'd been a couple hours since breakfast, and I'd played with Socrates down by the creek all morning.

"You'll grow up to be taller and thicker than a tree you keep eating the way you do."

Without further argument—amused, feigning annoyance—she melted a pat of butter in an iron skillet and dropped a piece of cold cornbread in to warm and crisp. She cut a hot dog into several pieces and scattered them around the cornbread, all of which sizzled, filling the kitchen with a pleasant charred, greasy aroma. She grabbed the jug of milk from the fridge and set it in front of me on the counter, then walked back to the stove.

"Pour yourself a milk," she said, flipping the cornbread over and reaching for her coffee.

"Can't I have some coffee?" I asked and looked at her, my jaw and eyes firm to let her know I was serious. I'd been building the question up inside myself all morning, chewing it over and over like a piece of gristle in my mouth.

Taking stock of me over the jittering edge of her mug as

she took a cautious sip, she deliberated and weighed my question. Finally, still not saying anything, she took another mug from the cupboard and poured it half full with coffee, added two teaspoons of brown sugar, and filled the mug rest of the way with milk.

"Here. Stir it good and don't tell Shawn I gave it to you. He'd skin us both alive."

I sat and sipped my coffee with what I hoped was an air of dignity. Holding the skillet's handle with a dishtowel, Flora scooped the cornbread and hotdog pieces out of the skillet with a spatula and dumped them on a paper plate. She handed me the plate and nodded.

"Don't suppose after you've eaten you'd want to help Mom carry some bricks to her garden would you?"

It was late winter, and Fern would want to have the new sections of her garden outlined with bricks embedded in the ground before spring came. With Shawn and me on the farm now, she'd need to plant more tomatoes, zucchini, green beans, and beets in the coming spring. She didn't try to provide us with everything we ate, but it was cheaper and, according to her, healthier to eat some homegrown vegetables with every meal. And she canned beets and greens beans for the winter, boiling them with generous amount of salt and butter, then sealing them carefully in. Thinking of how we'd eaten green beans with nearly every meal until we came down to the last Mason jar of soft, grayish-green mush, I couldn't bring myself to be excited about the prospect of Fern's garden, but I felt I owed her the biggest debt I could imagine for letting me into the adult world.

"Sure. I'll go get the wheelbarrow right now," I said, eager to prove myself.

"Keep your britches on. She'll be fine by herself for a bit longer. Just eat your food and drink your coffee." She patted my shoulder happily and turned back to her cleaning.

I tried to make heads and tails of what was going on around me—not so much right then, but over the past months on the farm, the bitterly earthy savor of coffee on my tongue.

9

Jeremy and Ray visited us in June. Shawn and the two of them transformed the farm into a circus. They played at competitions of every sort they could dream up. They threw horseshoes, did chin-ups from a low branch of the oak tree in the front yard, and arm-wrestled (both right- and left-handed). Flora and Fern scolded them for their immaturity, yet watched, captured by their boyish magic. Harold egged them on with taunts and smart-ass insults. We were all taken by their displays of tomfoolery. Ray suggested that we have a bonfire to go with the fireworks, which sounded to everyone like a pretty good idea. I spent most of the afternoon running all over the farm with a wheelbarrow, collecting branches, trash, pinecones—anything we didn't need that would burn. Harold decided to dismantle a wooden shed that hadn't been used in over fifty years. When we were done, there was a mound taller than Shawn and at least that wide.

"This fire's gonna singe God's short-and-curlies," Harold said. I nodded, though I had only the vaguest idea what short-and-curlies were. I sensed that he being somehow crude, and that Fern would have hit him with a dishtowel if he said it in the kitchen. I put away cornbread, buttered corn-on-the-cob, chiliburgers, fried hominy. Shawn, Jeremy, and Ray drank beer after beer, partaking in some unspoken race. Harold drank expensive scotch and water. Fern refilled her blackberry brandy many times, though everyone went along when she called each consecutive drink her third.

Darkness came on slowly and Shawn went to the barn and brought back a muddied, red plastic gas jug. He dowsed the edges of the pile and poured a gushing amount into the heart of what would become a ten- or twelve-foot fire hot enough, Harold claimed, to deform iron. After much gasoline and several dozen sheets of rolled newsprint, the fire burst to licking and dancing life. Shawn's stubble-covered face was sharpened and elongated by shadows, making a comic book vigilante of him. A fiery blossom wavered in Harold's scotch. Darkness crept between the green blades of grass and filled the space between trees. Leaves shimmered orange from the fire's glow. Coyote barks from the distance echoed off our houses. It might have been a scene out of one of my horror novels, except it was strangely comforting.

"How many shells've you got, Ray?" I heard Shawn ask.

"Enough to blow that damn pile acrossed the creek."

Proud laughter.

I was excited and confused. I knew something was about to happen. I looked on as the boys laughed and Harold shook his head, pretending disapproval.

"Hey, Shawn, does that burning permit you got include shotgun blasts?"

"This is my land. I don't need anyone's permission to shoot on my own land," Shawn said.

And to prove he didn't need anyone's permission he walked, straight-backed, to his truck, opened the door, and leaned in to get his 20-gauge and a box of shells. For that brief moment when he was half-consumed in the belly of the cab, the yellow light glowing through the windshield, I felt like we were in a movie or a book—or maybe more like we were a painting, frozen in the colors and shadows of that fire-lit night. It was a feeling I didn't want disturbed, but Shawn climbed back out and slammed the truck door.

The boys passed the shotgun around, taking turns shooting into the bonfire. We all jumped after the first shot hit the pile, sending a puff of blackened wood shards up through the pillar of flame. Fern grabbed me by the shoulder, pulled me back. Ray took the shotgun from Shawn, as though it was his right to shoot next. The slick clicking sound of a pump. Then the roar of buckshot being fired, and the explosion of wood and flame. Then it was Jeremy's turn. They went round and round, three-four times, like that. Harold twitched, wanting to join, but instead poured himself another scotch, adding water from the outdoor hose to cut it. Each shot was less surprising than the one before it, until it seemed that the world had always been full of heated explosions and earsplitting roars.

When they stopped, the field lay silent. Hollow. Scattered embers breathed orange-black breaths in rhythm with the breeze. The coyotes had quit their barking. Even the bugs—that constant rural soundtrack of chirping, squeaking, rattling—had ceased. No one said anything for what, in memory, seems like minutes. It was Ray, I think, [*since Ray was incapable of silence, I imagine it was Ray*] who first broke the pact with what had just happened.

"If there's a heaven, boys," he said to Shawn and Jeremy, "it'd better be just like this."

I resented that he'd left the rest of us out. As if old men, children, and women would have wanted a different paradise—or that we would be barred from heaven entirely.

Shawn crossed his arms over his chest, surveying the scene. It was then that it struck me that he'd called this his land. I didn't know the logistics of ownership, mortgages, and such, all of which probably did, legally, make this farm his land, at least in part. Despite what law said though, the farm was, to my mind the property of Harold and Fern. Over the years I learned how strained the farm finances were, considering Flora's constant need for medical attention and occasional surgeries. I have wondered, at my most cynical moments, whether Shawn wasn't lassoed in just to help pay the bills. Guilt and shame instantly follow thinking that, but I have thought it.

Jeremy began lighting fireworks, and even let me light several. Sparkles fluttered down from the neon explosions. I felt a tingle of fear every time I lit a wick, jerked back faster than necessary, then waited, tense, as the red glow devoured the ever-shortening wick. I glanced occasionally to the pile of fireworks, dreading their eventual disappearance. My pleasure at each separate explosion was all out of proportion with the circumstances, as was my dread—as if the short-lived glowing joys and the steady decrease of these gaudy, store-bought fireworks were some cryptic message; and if I could only understand it, I might be able to fix something.

My odd reverie ended when Ray finally saw the bats that

flew around the light poles. Harold built bat houses to attract bats to the farm. Even that far out in the country there are huge light poles (that sometimes double as telephone poles). "The lights attract the bugs. The bat houses attract the bats. The bats eat the bugs. The bugs do not eat your tomatoes. Simple as arithmetic," Harold explained, making small, punctuating gestures with his pipe.

But for Ray—whom I had never liked, and cannot remember one good thing the bastard ever did—the elegant, linear simplicity of why one might want bats on the farm was obscured in a darkness of willful stupidity. He was fiddling with Shawn's 20-gauge one second, and the next minute he was shooting at the bats, which were, luckily, too small and dark to make easy targets. At first, we assumed this was simply more Fourth of July tomfoolery. It wasn't until he yelled, "I got one!" that Harold realized what he was doing.

Protective of his bats, Harold chided him, "You stupid sonuvabitch. Put that gun down. What in hell do you think you're doing?"

"Shootin bats. What's so wrong with that?" Ray looked around, letting his eyes stop on Shawn, hoping for someone to talk sense to this old coot. Shawn let his head droop and looked at his shoelaces, turned suddenly into a schoolboy by his friend's—and therefore also his—mistake.

Ray fidgeted briefly, confused. Then, like a bull regaining his footing on uncertain ground, he marched, showily brazen, and picked up the dead bat. Everyone was silent as he tossed the corpse onto the bonfire. In his indignation Ray was too forceful, and the bat bounced from a center log and landed on the edge of the fire, where its hair and thin membranes burned slowly away. Shrunken and burnt, the bat looked like a shriveled human being.

10

Now I have to try to write about the first hospital stay. The build up to it I'll write later. That's not really important. It's the hospital that's important. The books on writing I got from the university library advise to cut all things that don't matter, focus on the intense scenes, and so on. I think the buildup will have to end in a surprise. It should be a major disruption in the story. Or something unexpected. Something like that story from Best American Short Stories where the kid masturbates into the decapitated torso of his sister's Barbie. Nothing that grotesque, but something true and utterly fucked-up like that, but here it wouldn't fit with the overall narrative at all, which would work as a sort of x-factor in the overall piece. I guess the first time I masturbated would have to have been around this time. That could be useful. And the quasi-incestuous aspect would titillate a certain type of reader, I guess.

Also, I need to find a way to get Flora's medical records. I can't remember when she was in the hospital, whether it was before or after certain events. I need to figure out the exact dates so I can get my chronology right. And I bet there would be all kinds of information I didn't pick up on back then. I could maybe even just recreate the entire document within the novel. For some reason, I always like it when writers do that. But what are the legalities of requesting a dead person's medical records? I bet Shawn will have to get them for me, since I am not technically related to her (with the medical issues and then her death, Shawn and Flora never got around to having her adopt me). It will be hard to explain to him why I want them.

I could also contact medical researchers who work with dystonia. I can ask the faculty in the Neuroscience Program here at University of Illinois. I bet David Littlefield will know who to ask, since he's dually appointed in the Psychology Department and the Neuroscience Program. I'll see if there are any useful medical facts I can get from them, but I still need to figure out when Flora was in the hospital.

Also, I should go back to the farm, take some photos, see how much has changed. Who still lives around there that I might know? I can hear them now. Ain't that the Wallace boy? The one whose daddy married Flora, bless her heart. Whatever happened to them? They just up and moved, not a forwarding address or anything. Took that little baby girl, sold the farm, and just left. What the hell *is he doing back here? People do the damnedest things.*

Anyway, yeah…tons of shit to get done if I am ever going to finish this thing.

11

Pinching the skin on my forearm—just hard enough to hurt a little, then letting go—I tried to remember everything I knew, scientifically speaking, about mirrors. The hospital waiting room smelled sterile the way hospitals do. Flora had been there three days. This was the first time I'd come to visit, the first time I'd been in a hospital at all since my mother had died. I looked out the window to the parking lot, tried to find our car; but it was pre-dawn and too dark to distinguish from the crowd of bumpers and hoods which one was ours. The translucent reflection of my face and my arm on the back of the green scratchy sofa floated on the window. I squinted and moved my head back, hoping that by some trick of the eye I could place my reflection out in the parking lot or in the field beyond, outside this room.

I pinched my arm again and watched the small patch of skin turn white, then go slowly red from the center out. The dull itchy surface of the sofa on the underneath of my arm complemented the sharp sting on the topside. There was an old man with loose bloodless skin sitting alone on the other side of the room. He'd walked up to the help desk and asked something I couldn't hear and returned disappointed several times. I felt sorry for him and tried to imagine what might be wrong with his wife or child. I considered moving closer so I could eavesdrop the next time he went to the help desk.

I thought of the last time I was in a hospital. My mother had spent the last weeks in the hospital back in Columbus. The sleeping gown the hospital had issued her fit well enough when she first arrived. By the time she died, she was constantly tugging at the edges of the gown, trying to get it to stay on her skin-and-skeleton frame. She was eaten up from her breast cancer, which had spread through her body, and from the treatments the doctors had put her through, I could barely recognize her as my mother. I often had the feeling that she wasn't my mother anymore. She was just the disease.

"You ready to go in?" Shawn asked and let his hand settle on my shoulder.

I didn't say anything, but I stood up, half-forgetting I was here to see Flora. Shawn led me down a well-lit bluish corridor—littered with empty wheelchairs and gurney carts loaded with bedpans and medications—then into a darkened sea-green room. Flora turned toward me and smiled. There were bruises on her arms from the IVs. I knew that's what the bruises were from because they looked just like the bruises my mother always had during her time in the hospital. The chemo and her cancer had made her veins weak, so the nurses had to use a different one every time, so she was covered in bruises. Seeing Flora's weak, spasming body, and seeing those bruises, made me want to cry. It really did.

Harold had said the night before how this seizure was worse than the last one from a few years back. He talked about the first one, not to anyone in particular, back when she was fourteen, how it was the scariest, and how since then she'd had the twitching and spasms. I wondered how I'd feel, what my classmates might do or say, if it was me who had it. I closed my eyes against the thought.

Shawn seemed nearly as shrunken as Flora. His face unshaven, his hair mussed and pressed at varying angles from the few hours of sleep he'd gotten, wearing the same clothes—he hadn't been to work or eaten properly since the attack. I'd gone to school and done my daily chores as usual. I stayed with Harold and Fern in their house. Shawn stayed alone in our house or at the hospital.

"How's school?" Flora asked, her voice a small, dry croak.

"Fine, I guess."

Later that night, helping Fern make dinner, I walked outside to throw her compost pile in the bushes and looked up at the sky. I had seen but not truly noticed the difference between country sky and city sky at night. All the stars were so bright, and the sky was crowded to bursting it seemed, like an attic with untold numbers of shining memories. I wasn't sure then which I liked better, seeing things so clearly or having certain sights obscured by the light from other sources. I felt like the only lives that were real were ours, and I didn't want to feel our lives so intensely.

As I was about to fall asleep, I remembered Flora was alone in the hospital. I also remembered that Harold had told me (though I couldn't remember when) how, in the past, children with Flora's affliction would be sold to the carnival as sideshow entertainment. Or killed for being possessed by demons. I closed my eyes and said her name. I hoped she felt better being alone because of it. I said her name again and again—*Flora, Flora, Flora*—as I felt myself falling off to sleep, like a ragged piece of moss sinking slowly through dark water.

12

It was while Flora was in the hospital that I took my first real interest in her condition. I do not choose my words accidentally here. I was interested in her condition more than her. I wonder if Shawn would think that is true even today. After Flora's death, much like after my mother's, Shawn and I went through another sea change in our relationship; this time, a huge gray apathy opened up between us, a gulf neither of us could be bothered to bridge. He paid bills and performed all the legal duties of a father, but his interest, his real interest was in Anna, their daughter. But I am getting ahead of myself.

I ask myself almost every day I sit down to write this—What is it? A novel? A memoir?—why I am doing it. It gets in the way of my research and takes from what little time I have for a social life. I suppose I am doing it for the reasons anyone writes about dead people and events so far in the past as to be more personal myth

*than history. Whatever the hell those reasons are. And reading over
it, as I do every time I sit down at my computer, I see how jumbled
it all is still, how the things that happened make no more sense now
than they did when I was living them—even less so, since I have
forgotten so much and what I do remember comes to me out of
order and in flashes I have enough psychological training not to
trust as accurate.*

13

The assignment was to write three pages about what you
had done over summer break. What had I done? There was
the weekend at Aunt Lucille's house when we still lived in
Columbus. I'd seen a panther in the zoo and had ridden a
go-cart for the first time. My cousin, Reida, was sixteen and
very pretty in a bikini, so pretty all the boys in the
neighborhood wanted to play with me so they could watch
her sunbathe. "Look at those knockers," one of the boys had
said. "I'd sure like to get my hands on those." Even though I
didn't like them looking at my cousin that way and couldn't
understand why they would want to, I knew somehow that
I was supposed to agree with them—"I'd like to pour some
sugar on them," I said (I also didn't understand why you
would want to pour sugar on someone, or ask someone to
pour it on you, as in the Def Leopard hit I'd heard thousands
of times, but the other boys liked the reference and laughed,
which made me happy.) And I figured I probably shouldn't
write any of that in my three-page summary.

   Beginning school that year had been difficult for me. I
entered Casey County Middle School over a month late and
had to do make-up work. The other kids had already done
this assignment, just after they returned from summer break.
And here I was doing it at home, over Thanksgiving break.
There was something disorienting about the gap in time and
trying to remember. So much had changed in the last three
or four months. It seemed like years ago that I lived in

Columbus. I could barely picture the streets we had lived on, my old school, the Korean restaurant where we had eaten every Saturday night. I vaguely remembered the roadblocks and foot traffic during a home football game. And that's when it really hit me that I might never get back home. That Columbus was no longer my home. This place was. And that thought terrified me.

And now Flora was in the hospital. That had happened to me over the summer, was still happening to me, but I didn't want to write about that, so I wrote about driving to Columbus, about how Ohio State University was the second biggest university in the United States. Stuff like that, stuff that didn't really matter.

[*To hell with this stuff. I'm boring myself writing about being a kid in a classroom doing some stupid assignment. It's been nearly a month since I last opened this file on my computer, and now that I do open it, I write worthless crap.*]

14

After the surgery, Flora had several days of recovery in the hospital before she came home weak and looking more dead than alive. But Flora did not suffer from a lack of companionship. Fern was at the house all day, reading a magazine or cooking or doing the laundry—anything to be there. Some nights she'd lay out bedding for herself on the couch without saying a word. Harold would stand to leave, and she'd simply tell him goodnight and see you tomorrow. I can't say whether Shawn or Flora resented Fern's presence, but it was never questioned. She would wake before the rest of the house and have the kitchen smelling of coffee and bacon by sunrise. Shawn cut Flora's bacon into smaller pieces and tore her biscuits into a small pile of flowery debris before pouring gravy over them. She weakly lifted the fork to her mouth and chewed.

They had replaced the wires along her spine and the small

box implanted under the skin on her left side that sent electronic pulses designed to counter the garble her spine made of signals from her brain. The new skin graft covering the metal box implanted on her right side was red and scabbed, and the incision scars along the back of her neck, where they'd inserted the new wires, were pink and puffy. The hair-thin wires along her spine were wired to the box in her side, which sent a constant electric pulse to stabilize the chaotic signals her brain sent. Without them she would have been entirely bedridden, flopping and jerking constantly. This new system also came with a device that Flora carried in a small canvas pouch. She could turn the pulse strength and speed up and down via this carry-along remote control.

After breakfast Fern washed the dishes while I cleared the table. I scraped the leftover food into a bucket for Socrates. With my bag of books over one shoulder and the bucket of slop for Socrates, I skipped down the driveway and on down the gravel lane that lead out to the main road. When I got out in front of the barn, I began to oink loudly, my call for Socrates whose diet so resembled that of a pig's. He scooted from under the barn door and circled around the spot on the ground where I always dumped his breakfast, his tail wagging so hard the back half of his body seemed out of rhythm with the front half.

15

The above story reminds me that we too often forget that normal days happen in the lives of everyone. It's likely not worth writing out at length, since the only news is bad news, but many of my memories don't include Flora's disease at all, almost as if she didn't have it half the time or whatever, though of course that's not true. It's just a trick of memory, but it's still telling. It lets me know that much (most?) of the time I was living on the farm, I didn't even think about her disease or think of her as disabled. She was just a normal person and we were normal people doing more or less normal things. Though it could be said that this is also what makes the horror of the other times so tragic. We would get lulled into normalcy, into thinking everything was fine, and then she'd be back in the hospital, reminding us in the most brutal of terms that things were not normal.

And a corollary thought: There are other tragedies or sadnesses that go unnoticed too often in the lives of people with one great noticeable wound or disadvantage. Families with a member suffering from cancer still have to deal with infidelity, daily arguments, car accidents, and so on.

We focus so much on the singular tragedy that we forget the non-tragic but we also forget the thousand minor tragedies that befall any life. And it is this that gives us all our common humanity — the normal human suffering that occurs to us all, and the normal human happiness.

16

Shawn told me to bring hay from the barn out to the cows, a chore I part-loved and part-hated. Climbing the high, thin rafters of the barn to throw down the bales of hay was as much fun as a boy could have. But I harbored a deep, irrational fear for our bull, believing that all bulls were rage-filled, blind killers.

I tossed the bale over the barbed wire fence and climbed under. Then, with my pocketknife, I cut the two pieces of dirty-tan twined rope holding the hay in its bale. Harold had told me it was best to scatter the hay in a few separate piles, and well away from the fence so the cows wouldn't accidentally run into it. "Cows are about as smart as the patties that've made 'em famous," Harold would make a point of saying anytime he explained to me some intricacy of their proper care.

I edged out as far as I dared from the fence, always keeping my escape route in mind — over or under the barbed wire — and looking every direction in case that bull took a notion to come barreling over a hill toward me. Harold and Shawn soon picked up on my fear and began calling the bull Killer.

"Go on in there," Shawn would say. "But keep an eye out for Killer."

"Andrew's not scared of that old bull, Killer," Harold would say, then add, slowing his words and stretching them to comical length, looking at each of us gravely, "he just— has—a healthy—*respect*—for this bull—or any bull, for that matter." And we laughed, me included, which didn't mean I was any less afraid of the bull. Those years are odd ones to look back on. Some days I felt as adult as the others, and other days I wanted to crawl into bed with a warm glass of milk and ask what the hell everything was, because I was so often lost in the day's goings-on.

Throughout the day I worked harder than normal, relishing my memory of how the coffee tasted. Socrates ran in circles around me as I distributed hay for the cows. I threw handfuls of hay on his back, and he'd jump, twisting his mouth back toward the hay, to get himself free of it. Then he'd run up to me so I'd do it again. I scratched him behind the ears, looking for ticks out of habit. If I found a fat one, I'd step on it to see the gray skin crack and ooze red-black blood. Small ones I would've set on a rock and stabbed through with the point of my pocketknife.

He darted across the field, disappearing over one crest then appearing as a sporadic dot on the next. I made several trips back to the barn for more bales of hay which I spread cautiously. I was cutting the twine of the last bale, when I heard Socrates barking. I looked up and saw him running in tight circles around the bull; it was unclear at first whether he was chasing the bull or being chased. I yelled his name, but he ignored me or didn't hear. I imagined him being crushed under the bull's hooves, or gouged on the bull's horns and thrown into the air. Socrates stayed a mere foot or two away from the bull, barking louder and louder. I yelled again.

Socrates jumped, barking. He jumped again and nipped

at the bull's side. He jumped, and when he landed, the bull lunged toward him, trying to butt him with his hornless head. Socrates jerked to the side and got tangled in the bull's hooves. The first one came down against Socrates' side, forcing out a high-pitched yelp. Then another came down on his snout, crushing it, sending a splatter of teeth and blood. The bull went down on its chest, then clumsily lurched back to all fours.

I yelled Socrates' name. "Socrates," I yelled. "Socrates." I was sobbing, I think. It's hard to remember. What I do remember is the moment I realized I was still in the field with the bull. I dropped my knife and the string I'd been uselessly clinging to and ran. I remember the jerky image of the field, the barn, brown water in the creek on the other side of the driveway. And the thud of hitting the ground. I was tangled in the fence and yelling Socrates' names, Shawn's name, just yelling noises. The barbed wire was in my thigh and side, but I flailed and tried to get up, and when that didn't work, tried to scoot farther away from the bull I was sure was barreling toward me. I imagined the bull's hooves pounding on my back and cried.

It was minutes later that Shawn was pulling me to my feet, carefully untangling the barbed wire from my flesh and clothes. I asked him if Socrates was dead. He told me to hush and stand still so he could get me untangled. I asked where the bull was, and he told me to hush. "Everything is okay now," he said.

17

And now the part I have dreaded writing the most, though I have no idea why I continue writing here at all. I should think more about that. Is it merely habit now? Or something more? But also, why have I grown frustrated with this project, working on it less and less. Just last week, Simone told me she'd noticed I spend less time typing at the computer, a gentle way of asking if I had given up, and I shrugged, saying simply, "Hobbies come and go."

18

When I got home from school, Shawn wasn't waiting for me at the end of the driveway as he usually did, but I thought nothing of it, since some days he was too busy or was called into work and couldn't be there. I kicked a flat hocky-puck-shaped rock in front of me on my way to the house. By the backdoor I set the jar of grasshoppers I'd taken to school for extra credit in science class. I would let them free after I changed into my work clothes. Inside, everyone was in the dining room. It was strange that Shawn and Harold would both be in the house at this time of day. This was the time, before Shawn went to work in town and after I got home from school, when we did most of the chores around the farm. I had the feeling they had been here for a while, waiting for me. I let my book bag fall to the ground and stepped tentatively into the room.

Shawn put his hand on my shoulder and said, "Andrew, you'd better sit down."

I hated the way that sounded, so condescending and straight out of a midday soap opera or B-movie, but I sat down like he asked, like I was a character in a stupid TV show. Fern frowned, just a ghost of a motion, a mild twist on the corner of her mouth. I remembered the jar of grasshoppers I'd set by the door on my way in. I'd taken them to school for extra credit in science class and was going to let them free after I'd changed into my work clothes.

Shawn finally started, "Andrew, we wanted to all be here when you heard. It'll maybe come as a shock, and it might change things around here a bit, quite a bit, frankly—"

Flora made a slight slurping noise, sucking an excess of saliva back into her mouth, a habit I'd grown accustomed to, didn't even notice much anymore, but right now it seemed disgusting. "What Shawn's saying is," (she sucked at her teeth again), "is that we're going to have a baby. We're all excited, me especially, since the doctors had said it wasn't possible."

"And frankly," Shawn said, "we just wanted you to know how good a thing this is for us, all of us."

Since Shawn and Flora met, I had felt somehow second choice, despite Shawn's insistence that a man's love for his wife was entirely different from his love for a son. Now it was even worse. I felt replaced, an old model easily discarded.

"That's great," I said. "I'm going to go outside."

"Andrew—"

"I'm going to go do some chores. I have to earn my keep more than ever now, huh?" I said, savoring the meanness of it, and went to my room.

"Let him be," Harold said.

I slammed my door. I could still hear them talking, but I couldn't make out what they were saying. But I didn't give a damn about what they were saying. All I wanted was for Shawn to come to my room and beg my forgiveness, which I wouldn't give. I would ignore him no matter how long he begged, until he gave up and walked away defeated. I changed my clothes and went out the back door, avoiding the living room. When I opened my door, they became silent as rocks. And imagined their grimaces as I let the screen door slam shut behind me.

Outside, I went directly and purposefully to work. We had dug up smooth slate from the creek bed over the weekend to line the edges of the driveway in hope that it would prevent the gravel from washing away when the late spring rains came. If we could reduce the wash-away, we'd save a bundle by not having to re-gravel the driveway every year or two. The slabs of smooth, gray rock were heavy, but I lifted and threw them into the wheelbarrow with pleasure. The strain of it calmed me, and I talked to myself—or rather, I had an imaginary argument with Shawn. My insults and cuts grew harsher and, with the added precision allowed by self-editing, I outwitted him, swatting his flat comments away with razor-sharp retorts. My acidic cruelty burned him to nothing, a patch of grease on the ground where once there was a man. As the lifting calmed me, the petty festering kept my hurt and frustration alive, so that I would forget my anger briefly and just enjoy the physical activity, then remember all that was said and hate this farm and this life more than before.

I pushed the now-full wheelbarrow to the end of the driveway to begin. I laid the slabs with care, placing each slab end to end and filling in gaps with smaller chunks of slate. I looked down the length of the driveway and felt despair at the scope of the project before me; the driveway must have been nearly a quarter of a mile long including the section between the two houses. Shawn and Harold were leaving me to my own thoughts. All three of us would be working on it from now on, but even so, it seemed an impossible task. I remembered, from my readings at the library, about the Norse tribes' belief in the afterlife. They believed that the only way to make it to Heaven, which they called Valhalla, was to die in battle. Then, while you feasted in Valhalla, you also trained for Ragnarok, the final battle between Good and Evil, a battle you were destined to lose. It seemed hopeless. Why would you waste your life being brave and honorable so you could go to Heaven to train for a battle you'd lose? It didn't seem like much of a reward for so much effort. With every stone I laid I imagined I was Thor battling the dragon I knew would kill me. This game of imagination kept me occupied, and after an hour of it, I realized that I wasn't thinking about Shawn anymore, and though it might sound weird, I wondered whether I should start hating him again or keep on with my little reverie about Thor and Asgard. It struck me as odd that I might choose to be angry or not. I decided to not think about the baby anymore right then.

Around seven o'clock Fern yelled to me from the back porch. It was time for supper. I rolled the wheelbarrow into the barn slowly, trying to waste time. I was nervous about going into the house. The things I had said would still be there, haunting the rooms like unseen ghosts. I searched my mind for some way to prevent or escape the awkwardness I'd feel when I went inside. I walked up the driveway a bit, looked back to survey my work, and continued forward. I noticed a blue piece of glass I'd seen earlier, on my way in after school. I suddenly remembered the grasshoppers I'd meant to let free of their jar. I sped up my pace. I'd poked air holes in the lid of the jar, I reminded myself. They should be fine. When I reached the edge of the porch, where I'd set the jar, I saw that it was no longer in the shade like it had been a few hours previous. I unscrewed the lid quickly to find four green, jagged corpses. I dumped them out on the lawn and screwed the lid back on. Tears welled up along the bottoms of my eyes. They're just bugs, I consoled myself, but I couldn't stop thinking about how they'd died, exposed to too much sun and too little air. Cooked and suffocated. Because of my carelessness.

I hadn't noticed Shawn was beside me. When I did, I turned toward him, not knowing what to say. He saw the wetness in my eyes.

"It'll be okay," he said. "Having a little brother or sister won't be so bad, will it?"

I looked to the spot where the grasshoppers lay, spindly legs and claw-like feet scattered in every direction, their empty black eyes gazing nowhere.

19

The thing that amazes me now is how disconnected I feel from all of this. The little boy with his petty jealousy, the workaday activities of the farm, the schoolmates I had—all of it—seems like someone else's story.

I didn't pay attention to the sale of the farm, but reading over what I've just written, I realize I still thought of the farm as belonging to Harold and Fern, who have both been dead for nearly a decade. Did it hurt Shawn to sell it? Did some part of him see it as his last connection to Flora and her childhood home, her family, their marriage together? I was in college when it happened, freshman year, and had other concerns. I remember thinking of it

*as a large and somewhat complicated bank withdrawal or
something like that. I am sometimes amazed at how selfish (or at
least self-centered) I can be. Even the indulgence of writing this
thing all these months, even as infrequently as I do now, seems
pathologically self-obsessed. I should spend this time doing nice
things for Simone or raising money to cure diseases like dystonia
instead of merely writing about them.*

20

July was moist and green. The heat raised a mist that
shimmered golden-green in the dark trees along the edge of
the creek. Bright, hot sunshine pushed through the leaves
and rested heavily on every surface. In June, when we were
worried that there'd be a drought, we dug craters—seven
feet wide, two feet deep—at random intervals along the creek
in order to catch as much of the flowing water as possible.
The cows drank from that creek. Creating reservoirs could
save us from having to pay for water to be trucked in from
the lake if the summer turned out to be a dry one. After three
weeks without rain, and the June sun bleaching the field
grass, the sky opened up and it rained in soaking torrents.

Up and down the valley there was a festive mood. Farmers
hosted barbeques and invited all their neighbors. Much food
and beer were consumed. After a month of regular rains, the
lake was full, the creek was broad and swift, and the crops
would be healthy enough to survive if August turned out to
be dry. A drought that summer would have meant more debt
in the form of subsidized loans; at least one marriage would
have broken up; more fights would have erupted at the bars
in Liberty.

The plastic of the lawn chair was almost unbearably hot.
It had been in direct sun all morning. Beneath my t-shirt
the skin on my back was tight from sunburn. Flora
wondered out loud again whether heatstroke could cause
a miscarriage. Harold assured her that his mother had

worked in worse heat than this while she was pregnant with him. Flora was in no danger sitting in the shade. "The only danger you're in is you might choke on an ice-cube from your glass of lemonade there."

Flora took a drink. Beads of condensation rolled down the light green glass and dropped onto the wood of the deck, which absorbed the moisture greedily, leaving darker brown patches that disappeared within minutes of exposure to the heat. I stepped into the shade and poured myself a half glass and emptied it with one gulp, then turned to go.

"You'd better get to work on those cans," Harold told me.

"Are we still going into town to sell them?" I asked.

My main source of income was the sale of aluminum cans. I would walk up and down the country roads where drivers tossed Coke cans and beer cans from their windows. Once a month Harold drove me into Liberty to sell what I'd collected. I had developed a passion for comic books, and my recycled can industry provided me a monthly supply of Spider-Man, Fantastic Four, X-Men, and Thor.

"Sure. And we'll stop by the Dairy Queen to get us some milkshakes," Harold said. "Maybe we'll all go in together." He looked to Flora.

"A milkshake's exactly what I need for this heat," Flora said.

"Well, Andrew, you'd better hurry with those cans or else Flora here will have your ass in a sling."

I ran off in mock fear. Laughter rose and sank behind me.

An hour later I had three trash bags full of crushed cans. Against regular practice, we drove the farm truck into town. I threw the cans in the bed of the truck and wondered briefly if they would fall out on the ride. But Harold didn't say anything about it, so I stopped thinking about it. Fern decided not to come with us. She was expecting a friend to pick her up for bingo night down at the church. They were going to eat dinner in town before the big game. (It was the last one of the month, when all winnings are double, a fact that had Fern bustling.) I felt a twinge of loss at not being able to go to the library while she played. The last game of the month always went later, granting me a longer stay in the library stacks.

Whatever loss I felt was outweighed by the impromptu adventure of driving the farm truck into town for something so frivolous as a milkshake. Farms can be business, business, day in and day out, making any frivolity a treat.

Shawn was at work, so it was just the three of us. The side of my knee touched Flora's, a fact she either didn't notice or didn't care much about, but it pleased me, the sensation of closeness. My thighs stuck to the hot plastic seat, and there were cracks where the foam was coming out that I picked at the whole way there. Harold told us stories about friends of his from years ago. He told us about when he was a drill sergeant for the army how one trainee had been hit in the back with a rubber bullet during an exercise and suffered a shattered vertebra because of it. Apparently the young soldier-to-be had gotten something like eight thousand dollars in compensation and life-long disability checks that didn't quite pay rent.

But before the mood could deaden much, Harold changed the subject by telling a joke.

"Okay, there's this man at a bar. Now, this is a special bar, seeing as it's located on the top of Mt. Everest; gotta be flown in there by plane, big-time tourist attraction. And he's ordering whiskeys right and left. Every so often he gets up and goes to the window, opens it, steps outside onto the thin air and floats like there's nothing to it.

"After about the third time he does this, another man at the bar (a tourist from out of town who doesn't know any better) asks him how it is he does that. The first man says it's the upward air currents that are so strong they can hold you up. He tells the other man there's nothing to fear. He goes to the window and demonstrates how safe it is by doing it a couple of times.

"The second guy finally works up his courage to do it. He opens the window, looks down, shakes his head, then steps out. He falls ten thousand feet to his death: *SPLATT!*

"The bartender looks at the first man and says, 'You sure are a mean drunk, Superman.'"

I laughed at that so hard that my face began to hurt.

[*That trip into town is the last happy day I can remember from the years I spent on the farm.*]

21

Summer finally came to an end, and school started. It was my first year in high school. I'd heard stories of kids smoking weed in the parking lot; girls who gave blowjobs behind the bleachers; hulking athletes who beat the hell out of freshmen like me—the usual compendium of half-truth, urban legend, and cheap cliché. And all of my middle school teachers warned us that things were going to be harder, that we couldn't be our usual lazy selves and hope to make it in high school. High school. It sounded like a foreign country, not the two redbrick buildings I'd driven by hundreds of times over the past few years. I wanted to be popular, and I wanted to be the best student in school, though I knew those two things didn't usually go together.

I signed up for advanced biology and chemistry classes, even though as a freshman at Chatham County High, I was only required to take one science that year. I also enrolled in Beginning Latin. I don't remember when I'd decided to become a doctor, but by my first day of High School, I was already planning my course load to look good for medical school. I had read in one of the brochures from the advising office that Latin could prove useful for students who wanted a future in medicine or law. I walked into the halls of the school full of daydreams about being an ace surgeon, curing diseases, and long hours working with appreciative blonde nurses.

On Harold's advice, I also went to the interest meeting for the school newspaper. The other students were amiable enough, and there was, I found, a sizable overlap among those students in the advanced science classes and the school newspaper. This was due less to any overlap of interest than to the general urge to be a good student. Whatever it was that looked good on their transcript, they would do, and their personal interests weren't necessarily a concern, unless you counted the interest we had in seeming smarter than other students and the desire for scholarships for college. [*This impulse did end up serving me well, I guess, since I ended up with a scholarship to attend the University of Kentucky for undergrad, and then I received the largest fellowship at the University of Illinois which then hired me on after my PhD. Never underestimate the combined powers of a fragile ego and enormous personal ambition.*]

22

As the pregnancy progressed, Flora's dystonia progressed with it. She dropped things. Her speech was harder to understand. Her spasms and muscle cramps were more severe. Eventually, she was unable to get out of bed. She had been going in for weekly visits to the hospital. Seeing her in her chair—that's how I thought of it, her chair, and never sat in it even when she was in bed or out of the house—I was amazed by her wherewithal. I'd overheard Fern telling Shawn that though she didn't approve of it normally, maybe Flora should consider ending the pregnancy. [*It was only later, when in health class we discussed abortions, that I understood what Fern had meant.*]

But there was something else that I felt as I watched her sit there, towel resting on her chest to catch the drool that all but continuously poured from her limp mouth. I was disgusted by her. She wore diapers like a baby because her motor control had deteriorated to point of shitting herself. Half-chewed food fell onto her towel and Fern quickly scraped it back onto the plate and fed it to her again. And when she spoke, it was like a zombie from a horror movie, all moaning vowels and no meaning. It made me feel guilty to be disgusted, knowing how much she was suffering for the child she was carrying. It was out of a mixture of guilt and disgust that I avoided her as much as possible during those months.

23

October came in like a lamb, the leaves a pleasant autumnal array and the air redolent with dried fields and wildfires, but it left roaring — thunderstorms, winds, and in first weeks of November sleet and freezing rain. On the day Flora's caesarian section was scheduled, the long gravel driveway that ran through the farm and to the main road was a treacherous mix of ice and mud. Flora had initially wanted a natural birth, but her doctor warned her that long hours of labor would have unpredictable effects on her condition, and after much pleading on Shawn's and Fern's part, she had finally given in. I could see that she was scared, and that fear led her to taking what the doctor assured her was the safer route. Everyone was relieved by her decision.

They set the date for the c-section, and things proceeded smoothly. The baby, a girl according to the ultrasound, was developing healthily. [*I was unable to imagine the baby having a gender until it was born, at which point it would become a she, but not until then.*] Her name was going to be Anna Marie. The others went around talking about the baby as if she were already born. "How's little Anna doing today?" Fern would ask, and coo something at Flora's swollen belly as though the baby could hear her. Or, Shawn would bring home supplies to make a crib and say to no one in particular that Anna can't wait to see her new crib.

24

The university is closed today due to a blizzard here in Illinois, so I have just been sitting at my kitchen table, typing in an unfocused way. Now I'm typing to you, or myself, or whatever. You get the idea. I hit a roadblock in the writing and wanted to call Shawn for some reason. All this writing about our family and the past has me thinking of him more than I have in years. It also has me thinking about other people's families, which basically reminds me how I am totally estranged from my own. I never talk to my half-sister except on Christmas. I don't send her birthday gifts, and I'd forget it's her birthday at all except that I have it listed in this birthday reminder program I have for my computer.

So why am I writing this? I've given up on ever actually finishing it. I see no purpose in putting the effort into it and publishing it and getting, what?, maybe a few thousand dollars. Maybe. I am just writing this for myself, and I can't even be bothered with it most of the time. It makes me wonder why we are drawn to writing, especially writing about ourselves. One of the common attacks on certain kinds of writing, especially political plays or poems, is that writing a sonnet or whatever about the plight of the Palestinians will do nothing to change the plight of the Palestinians. True enough, but I submit to you that writing a poem or a novel-memoir-thingie about your fucked up childhood and shitty relationship with what's left of your family won't do much to correct that situation either.

So it seems that only the utterly delusional write fiction or poetry to change the world anymore. I mean, Steinbeck and Solzhenitsyn were able to do it, but today it is only the rarest of novels that changes public opinion. An op-ed column in the town newspaper would go further to changing whatever you feel is wrong with the world. I guess if you could make hundreds of thousands of dollars on a book and donate it all to a foundation researching some illness, dystonia for example, you could do some good. If I were to ever finish this book, that's what I'd do, donate all the money to some foundation. But even that makes little sense. I could make more money teaching a few extra summer classes and donating that money; and it would be more or less certain I could get the classes, whereas the odds on publishing this approach nil.

But since I know I will never finish it and don't even care anymore if I finish it, then why I am still sitting at my desk typing at this and listening to Simone showering in the bathroom? Perhaps more importantly, why do I want to know why? People keep diaries, scribble little ideas to themselves, makes notes for letters or books or whatever, all the while knowing nothing will ever come of it.

The answer could be simply that we constitute ourselves in and with and through language, and by producing more of it and in a clearly formulated way, we feel ourselves more fortified in our constitution—we feel more real. Or maybe it's just cheap art therapy; the talking cure but reshaped into the typing cure. At any rate, it is about us, not about the world, no matter the subject matter; well, at least what I have been writing is about me and not about any disease or any other people except tangentially. That might not be true for some books I've read. I can concede that. But for me this process is about understanding me and my world, even if I am imagining the other people who live in it with me. Hmmm. Is that true? It feels true. I'll have to think about it more later.

For now, I am going to write about Flora at the onset of her dystonia. It occurred to me the other day that when her symptoms started, she was almost exactly the age I was when I met her. I am not the sort of person to draw any meaning from that. It struck me is all, so I want to try to imagine what it was like for her. Maybe get me out of my own life for a bit. And since this is just a journal now, nothing the world will ever see, I can do anything I like. There is freedom in that. Simone was right. When I was thinking of myself as a writer, I was taking this shit much too seriously. I was trying to write something that could be recognized as a novel or memoir, instead of putting down my thoughts in a way that mattered to me. Suddenly I feel very sorry for writers and how constrained their work must be by such concerns.

But on to Flora, years before I met her. I had thought about writing this in first person, but I think I'd better give myself the distance and mobility third person allows.

25

Eager to be with Flora, Harold didn't notice that Fern had removed herself to the farther reaches of the house or farm, always being helpful but never bringing herself too close to Flora's bedroom—as if she were avoiding a contagious patient, though she knew Flora's condition wasn't contagious.

That, if nothing else, the doctors could tell them for certain. It wasn't fear for herself that kept Fern away in those first weeks after Flora's seizure, the first weeks of their "new life" as a nurse had called it (an absurdly positive-sounding phrase for being thrown into a pit of snakes, Fern thought). No, what kept Fern away was an unwillingness to accept the newness of everything. She simply wanted her daughter just as she had been. Some mothers will say that their daughters are perfect but secretly think they should be taller or cruelly point out that they didn't get the family bosom, but not Fern. She had never wished her daughter taller, thinner, smarter, shapelier. She only wanted her to be happy and long-lived. Fern's sole selfishness may have been her extended daydreams about grandchildren, though she didn't feel that was unnatural. Seeing your grandchildren born was somehow the completion of a cycle.

Harold may not have noticed his wife's absence, but Flora did. It took only a matter of days for her to notice the pattern: Fern preparing everything—cooking each meal, washing bed linen and clothes, picking vegetables from the garden—and Harold bringing whatever Flora might need to her, as though performing odd diplomatic missions within the household. She lay, only slightly twitching relaxed as she was from the Valium Doctor Page had prescribed. Harold was reading to her from his favorite novel, *Cannery Row*, when she interrupted him.

"Where's Mom?"

"Probably out in the garden. I saw her going that way a while back. You need something?"

"I was just wondering where she was."

Harold wasn't sure if he should continue reading.

"I'm feeling better," she lied. "Let's go somewhere, out on a drive or something."

"You know what the doctors said." Every detail of their daily lives now seemed dictated by what doctors said.

Doctor Page had advised them to keep Flora at home, mostly in bed, for a few weeks, until she had regained her strength. There was no way to determine whether the spasms would stop, he said. They were still trying to diagnose the cause. After four days in the hospital and no signs of immediate danger to Flora's life and no further tests to be run just then, Doctor Page advised bed rest at home. He shook Harold's hand, more like a friend than a professional, and promised that he would call every neurologist he knew, that he would find a way to improve Flora's condition. There was something in the way Doctor Page held onto his hand and something in the warm, sad look in his eyes that made Harold trust this man with the well-being of his daughter.

"We could just go get some ice-cream in town, couldn't we?" Flora asked. "You, me, and Mom."

Harold worried about her being out in public, how others would treat her. He was not yet able to think the word *crippled* in relation to his daughter; he wouldn't let himself think of his daughter that way, *crippled*; it sounded too permanent.

"Sure. I'll go find your mother. Then we'll go and get us some ice cream," he said, loading his voice up with enthusiasm.

He nearly hopped off the bed, hoping to cheer Flora with his display of energy. He helped her out of bed and into several layers of clothes, more than was necessary considering the temperature. Then he left the room to find Fern.

When he didn't see her in the house, he peered through a window in the kitchen which faced the vegetable garden, but she wasn't there either. Walking toward the barn, yelling her name enthusiastically, using the voice of someone with good news to tell, Harold loosened his stride to something resembling a skip or a dance. He began singing.

> *I scream.*
> *You scream.*
> *We all scream*
> *for ice cream.*

He saw that the barn door was opened and figured Fern must be laying out hay for the cows, which he'd forgotten to do, even though she'd reminded him twice that day already. But he refused to let his oversight cloud his mood. He was rehearsing his thank-you to Fern, imagining the look on her face when he lifted her into the air and kissed her like a brazen teenager, savoring already her look of surprise at his suggestion that they go to the Dairy Queen in Liberty. What the hell, he'd say, we've certainly earned it.

The first sign he should have seen was her being in the loft, wrestling with a bale of hay, making it impossible for him to lift her into the air romantically. But his lighthearted mood had blinded him to omens. He probably attempted a joke or maybe a playful innuendo. Whatever he said, it was met with a flat look, almost a scowl. But still his mood would not falter. He tried another joke, this time about ice cream, which he now suggested they go get.

"Why?"

"What do you mean 'why'?" he asked, adding that ice cream was intrinsically good, as all wise philosophers and children knew. "In the great words of Plato: 'Ice cream is just goddamned good.' A rough translation from the original Greek, but I'm a farmer, not a professor." He chuckled at that, liked the way it sounded.

"What good is ice cream going to do any of us, Harold?"

He saw where this was going, and his invincible happiness began to crumble.

"Well, I thought it might do Flora some good to get out of the house," he said. "And I thought it might do us some good, too."

"You two go on alone."

"I wish you'd come," he said. "And I think it'd mean a lot to Flora."

Fern abandoned the hay bale and started down the ladder to where Harold stood, chewing his lower lip ruefully. He watched her back down the rungs of the ladder and, looking at her skin and the way she was moving, thought she resembled a turtle—a harmless, loose-fleshed, slow-moving reptile. He tasted blood from his lip where he'd bitten too deeply. He massaged the soft mound on his inner lip with the tip of his tongue, working a wet flap of skin free and spitting it out.

Fern was not a cruel person, though she knew how to be cruel. And she knew Harold perfectly, all of his soft spots and sensitivities, his naïve hopes, everything about him open to pain or embarrassment. When she got to the ground, she turned to face him, already huffing with frustration.

"Do you think that by pampering her you'll cure her?"

"She'll get better," he said, frowning. "That's the truth."

"The truth?" she asked, her voice letting him know that she doubted he knew what the word meant.

"We can't be negative about this..." he searched for the right word.

"*New life*?" Fern snorted.

"About her condition. Our daughter's condition."

"You two go on alone," Fern suggested. "Someone's got to keep up the work around here."

And so Harold and Flora went alone. As they went bumpily down the gravel driveway, Fern waved to them, but they didn't notice. Then, as Fern looked away, Flora turned her head toward where she was standing, staring at her feet. Fern went back to spreading hay for the cows. The sun burned in the distance on the flat of the horizon like a house ablaze, and the field disappeared into a watercolor wash of purples, oranges, and darkening greens.

26

Maybe I had the wrong idea from the beginning. Maybe I should have been writing about Flora the entire time—a sort of imagined biographical novel or whatever. Or maybe I could pull one of those Faulkner moves and give a chapter to each family member, telling all of our stories throughout our years together. So many possibilities. But I just received a large research grant, so free time to mess around here will soon be scarce. And then there's my and Simone's wedding to think about.

But for now, I am enjoying writing about Flora, so I will continue a bit longer.

27

The medical bills stacked up, and after several months away from school, Flora returned. There was discussion of home-schooling her, to protect her from the inevitable cruelties of her classmates and to have her near and safe. But Fern convinced Harold that Flora would have to learn how to interact with the outside world some day, that protecting her now would only make matters more difficult in the long run. Harold didn't like the idea, but he'd been working part-time with an old buddy of his who ran a body shop in Liberty, ten or so hours a week to make extra money, meaning he had less time. And maybe Fern was right.

At first, the children in school regarded her with a hushed curiosity. Old playmates didn't approach her, and when she looked to them, they looked down at the floor or out the window. The teacher, Mrs. Strand [*who was later my teacher*], had warned them about Flora's condition and had coached them as to how they should act toward her. She had issued threats as to how many times they would have to copy the Gettysburg Address by hand, her favorite form of punishment, if she heard one cutting remark or one snicker. If she even suspected that that they were making jokes at Flora's expense, she explained, they would be sitting in her room writing out Lincoln's speech every recess for a month.

Each day, after Flora was safely on the bus, Harold and Fern sat down to calculate their quickly worsening finances. They mortgaged and re-mortgaged the farm. Flora didn't think about the cost of her treatments. She concentrated on sitting still on the bus, which was impossible, and tried to ignore the stares and whispers. On her fourth or fifth day back to school, a boy she hadn't seen before sat beside her on the bus.

"Hey, my name is Joel," the boy said as though he'd been rehearsing it for a while. "You're Flora, right?" The words spilled from him.

"Yeah."

"Those are cool shoes you got there."

She didn't understand what this was about or where it was going, but she tensed, waiting for the jeering cruelty she knew was coming.

"So, are you going to keep doing track? You were real good."

"No, I don't guess so," Flora said, her speech slurring the last two words into one spitty mess. She thought this was the beginning. She felt a jolt in her stomach, a sudden hollowing jolt, and she almost started crying. She felt trapped in the bus seat, pressing herself against the wall and window, and the boy—what had he said his name was? George? John? Joel?—Joel was blocking her in. She squeezed her book bag to her chest. Her jaw spasmed and she bit her tongue. Her eyes were wet and her vision was blurry. She just knew she was going to start bawling any second no matter how hard she fought it.

"I'm sorry. I didn't mean to ask that," he said. "I'm sorry."

Flora stared at him.

"Do you want me to leave you alone?" he asked.

She hadn't expected him to ask that. It hadn't occurred to her that she had a choice in the matter.

"No. You don't have to."

They rode rest of the way to school not knowing what to say. Flora offered him a piece of gum [*or maybe a Tootsie Roll, something like that, I imagine*]. He chewed it with audible deliberation like it was the most interesting and tasty candy in the world. When the bus stopped in the school parking lot, Joel stood up and motioned for Flora to get out as he blocked the aisle with his body, protecting her from the push and shove of the other children. He walked with her into the school and through the hallways. When it was time to go to their separate homerooms, they looked at each, wondering for the hundredth time what to say.

"Well, see ya."

"Yeah, see ya."

[*I kinda like the ending here, their innocence and the underlying*

urge to be around each other despite not knowing how to act when
they are. I like "jeering cruelty" and "audible deliberation" as well,
but that's not the right language for kids this age. I'll have to go
back and change that at some point.]

28

It was mid-November and the farm's fifty acres were redolent
with autumn. She came down the hill carefully, letting one
cramped foot, then the other, feel the ground for placement.
The cool air made her cramping worse, more painful, but
she hadn't told her father about that yet. She just turned up
her electric blanket to its highest setting every night and let
the heat sooth her aching muscles. She hated that being
outside hurt her. She hated everything.

She used to explore the forest that covered some thirty-
odd acres, stretching ever more wildly toward the southeast.
And autumn had been her favorite time for this. Leaves
crunching underfoot, a bracing chill in the air, the possibility
of happening upon a doe sipping at the creek. She would
take her rucksack with her, containing a decades-old, leather-
bound copy of *The Flora of Kentucky*, her notebook, and the
charcoal pencils Harold had bought her to draw the trees,
rocks, and wildlife she found.

But she hadn't yet been in the forest all season. Harold
and Fern were reluctant to let her out of their sight, and the
idea of her navigating the crags and embankments seemed
impossible. She looked to her notebook, which she now used
for her exercises to learn how to write legibly again. Intricate
drawings of foliage and wildlife were a distant memory. She
didn't argue when her parents told her she should wait a
while before she went wandering around on her own.
Without being able to sit down and draw, her walks would
have lost some of their magic anyway.

Earlier in the day, doing her writing exercises, Flora
watched her hand and remembered the day in class when

her hand cramped so violently and she had screamed out. So, she thought, my entire body is one big writer's cramp. Thinking that had made her want to laugh, but instead she'd begun to cry. And now she was walking down the embankment, heading to her favorite spot, where large, dried vines draped over a stretch of Poplar Creek, and where she'd always gone to do her drawings and to read her books on animals and plants. She'd just gotten up from her exercise booklet, grabbed her coat and rucksack, and left the house without leaving a note or making any sound at all. She wanted to be alone. That was all she wanted. Ever since it had begun, there were doctors, nurses, lab technicians, preachers, neighbors, her parents, more doctors, more days in hospitals with nurses and preachers and parents—and all she wanted was to be away from it, to be alone.

She remembered Joel from the bus ride the previous day and imagined herself marrying him. He was the only boy in the school who didn't just stare at her or worse. But then she was sad because she'd have to marry a really rich man to afford all of her medical bills. And who would want to marry her anyway? Best not to even think about that. Flora felt bad that her dad was so worried about medical bills all the time. She hated going in for tests and more tests, especially a recent one, where they had taken bone marrow from her left arm. That had hurt so much she'd cried most of the day, stopping from time to time, until she moved or accidentally touched the arm or it just started hurting again for no reason. She hadn't been able to sleep for two nights because every movement in her sleep would wake her with a jolt of pain. She knew what bone marrow was, had seen diagrams of it in her school biology books. The word made her think of birds and their bones, which was weird, she thought, since birds had hollow bones, didn't have any marrow. Why would she think of birds then, if they didn't have any? That's stupid, she thought and was angry. She decided not to think about it anymore.

As she walked, Flora named the names of things. She saw a patch of honey locust trees and thought the word *honey locust*. She saw a sourwood, thought *sourwood*. Saw a pawpaw bush and thought of her father. She could feel the weight of the backpack. She would get to her spot soon, and then she would have to sit down and try to draw the things around her. She hadn't decided it before she left, but the whole way to her spot where the vines hung so pretty over the water, she knew she was going to try to draw them. She almost turned around and went back to house, back to her handwriting exercises. She thought maybe they wouldn't have even noticed she was gone. It'd be like she never came out here at all. But she didn't stop walking toward Poplar Creek. She didn't even slow down.

29

Flora died before I could forgive her for not being my mother. I think I had begun feeling connected with her, which is not the same thing as forgiving her, or liking her, but she was part of my life in these little integral ways. I wanted to like her or one day love her, because I knew this was what I was supposed to do eventually, but also because I knew she was a good person who wanted me to love her. There is no way to know this, of course, but I think by the end, she had taken me on as part of her family in that permanent way that can't be broken, no matter what kinds of distrust or dislike passes between people.

When I first started writing this, I was certain it was about getting to know myself, and later, after writing about my father, I was certain it was about working through that relationship, but now, after imagining Flora's childhood, I wonder if it hasn't been about coming to terms with Flora's life and death. Who gives a fuck what it's about though? It's just a bunch of words anyway. Likely the only useful thing to come of all this is that I plan to write a sizable check every year to the Disability Studies Program at Ohio State University. Those checks, and the work they will facilitate, will matter more than all of the pretty sentences in the world.

I have one more day to write about though, and then I can be done with this.

30

I woke up before everyone else. I'd slept in fits and, finally, I gave up trying around five a.m., opting to get up and eat some breakfast and study for the chemistry test I'd been worrying about all week. By that time in the school year, Ms. Spencer, the English teacher who served as advisor to the school newspaper had taken an interest in me and given me a copy of Hemingway's *Collected Stories*. I read each story two or three times, following along as Nick Adams had his adventures and failings and strange affairs. Hemingway's work as war correspondent also served to glamorize journalism and, by extension, everything I did at the school newspaper. [*Is Ms. Spencer's gift to blame for all the time I've spent writing this? Very possibly. At least in part.*]

At the same time, I was more determined than ever to become a doctor. [*I was in the early stages of that delusion.*] I reviewed medical dictionaries, anatomy texts, and studied my Latin. There was little time for history class, which I decided was unimportant in comparison to science's fact. And the stories we had to read for history class all seemed chintzy in comparison to the harsher reality depicted in Hemingway's work, and the way I figured, no one ever removed a tumor or delivered a baby by reciting how Columbus bravely sailed across the ocean blue to discover America. [*Though I did nostalgically enjoy saying Columbus's name, since it reminded me of Columbus, Ohio.*]

I poured myself a bowl of cereal and a glass of orange juice and sat at the kitchen table with my history book spread out, studying just the boldfaced terms, hoping to cram in as much information as I could manage with as little commitment as possible. As I sat there, mulling over terms like Magna Carta and Manifest Destiny, I thought about things that mattered in life, in the world. I came back again to my conviction to become a doctor, even though I couldn't remember exactly when I had decided on that as my career.

I would do neurology, I was certain.

On the bus I stared out the window, looking at the trees and fields and houses go by. I tried, but I couldn't make any of my favorite super-heroes fly or run along beside us. The bus went by Wendell's new barn, which was nearing completion. The red-vaned cupola on top showed just how much thought and effort he'd put into building it. He was going to have the best barn in the county, he'd boasted, and I believed him. I liked the idea that Wendell would have the best barn in the county. Even if I could have built a better one, I wouldn't have.

Then the barn was gone from sight. I leaned back and closed my eyes. The smell of the bus was overwhelming. The thick odor of diesel exhaust mixed with the warm plastic seat to make the air nauseating. I put down the window and took deep breaths of the cold, fresh air until Tommy Perkins began yelling to the bus driver, "Andrew has a window down!" In the winter months we were not allowed to open the windows for any reason, but in my need for breathable air, I hadn't remembered that. I was the last kid on the bus Mrs. Crowley expected to be breaking the rules.

"Andrew? Is everything alright?" she asked.

"Yes. Sorry. I just needed some air. I'm okay now," I said and slid the window back up. Tommy Perkins just grinned at me.

It was during biology, my favorite subject, when I was called to the principal's office. I stared at the intercom speaker as the message was repeated, the way they do over intercoms, and kept staring after it went silent. I looked at the door and then at Mrs. Wyatt. She nodded permission to go but didn't say anything.

Flora had been taken to the hospital the day before with a fever of 104°. She'd collapsed on the patio, unconscious. Harold heard the thump. When she wouldn't wake up, we drove her to the hospital in Lexington. Shawn sat stoically except that he was rubbing his hands together as though they were cold. I sat beside him, thinking how familiar hospitals had become. They had lost their air of panic. I'd spent so many hours wandering their halls—drinking the watery hot chocolate from vending machines, flipping through magazines on subjects I had no interest in—that they no longer felt alien the way hospitals should if your life is anything approaching normal.

Flora's fever was so high that they weren't sure of the cause of her unconsciousness. She might have hit her head when she fell—there was a bruise above her temple from the fall—or, what the doctors feared most, she might have brain damage from her dangerously high temperature. They had stripped her naked and blanketed her with ice packs when she arrived at the hospital. With the drive into town and the response time of the hospital staff, they figured the fever had been at those levels for just over an hour, maybe longer. Running a fever that high for that long can cause severe brain damage, and there was no way to determine her condition until she regained consciousness.

And so when I heard my name on the intercom, I knew it was about Flora and that it wasn't good. When I got to the principal's office, Shawn was standing there solemnly.

"We have to go to the hospital," he said. "The doctors say the whole family should be there through the evening."

The principal's office, which usually held an air of awe about it, being the center of all power at the school, was just a small poorly built room in a squat red-brick building.

"I'll be praying for you all, Mr. Wallace," Principle Durham said.

[*That day feels like three or four days in memory. The morning is a full day. The bus ride another day. Classes. The few minutes in the principal's office. And the drive to the hospital. Somehow they don't feel consecutive, as though they happened months apart, in no particular order. Also, on the drive to the hospital, I got carsick, which happened to me often at that age, and when Shawn pulled over to let me out for air, I vomited—and since that day, whenever I vomit, no matter the cause, I always think of that time I vomited. It has become some warped Platonic ideal of vomiting. I have never told anyone this, because there are few occasions in life to share such things. But every time, during college, when I would get too drunk and be puking my brains out, I would be transported back to the day Flora died; a few years ago, when I got food poisoning, same thing. I have no idea why I am writing this here, except perhaps because I know I'll never have another opportunity to express it.*]

I stood on the side of the road, throat convulsing with acid and school cafeteria food. I recognized chunks of the pizza I'd eaten, saw the brownness of the chocolate milk. It made me vomit more. I looked up, resting my hand on my knee. Shawn was looking at me with concern and impatience. The fumes from the car hit my face, and I thought I might start the vomiting again, but I didn't. I pictured Flora in the hospital, dying. I said out loud, food particles and spittle on my lips, "Don't be dead. Please don't be dead, you bitch."

31

I should have been dating these writing sessions. It's been — what? — six months since I wrote that last bit. Something like that anyway. My wedding is in two days. I don't need to aim the full force of my PhD in psychology at myself to see why I am reminded of this little abandoned project. Sometimes we are so transparent, no study and no analyst is needed. The strongest memories from my time with Flora belong to the wedding day I opened with. Which I was reminded of for obvious reasons. And then I couldn't resist ending with a wedding since I'd started with a wedding. Well, I guess I'm not ending with a wedding. But I'm mentioning one, building up to one, letting a hypothetical reader imagine one as the end of the story.

What's that one-line definition of tragedies and comedies? Tragedies end with a funeral, and comedies end with a wedding? Goethe or Shakespeare said that, I think. I guess I could Google to find out who said it, but it doesn't really matter who said it. I like it. *And I like the idea that I've written a comedy, not a tragedy. Not a comedy in the ha-ha sense but in the things-aren't-infinitely-shitty sense. And there's that other college instructor trick of describing the action of a comedy as a smile. Things start out good, on a high note—the first corner of a smile. Then things get bad, forming the crestfallen depth of the smile. Then things end on a (different) high note enriched by the travails of the narrative—thus the second corner of the smile. It's a nice little pneumonic, pedagogically useful and so forth, but my story doesn't quite form a perfect smile. With what Simone calls my grotesque humor, I am tempted to say it is more of a stroke victim's smile, with one side much higher than the other. We get the lift at the end, but it does not raise us as high as where we started. Consider the stroke victim: life is utterly changed, for the worse, and in ways he does not yet understand. Everything is unstable; tragedy, as it were, could strike at any time, leaving him with even less mental and motor function—with a less uplifted smile, one might say (if one had a grotesque sense of humor). But the fucker is still smiling his lopsided smile, and that's got to be worth something, doesn't it? We have to pretend it is at any rate, whether we believe it is or not.*

And so I will marry Simone. I have invited my father and half-sister. We will all act like a happy family. Hell, we'll be a happy family for a day. And the feeling of that will be what I remember for months to come. I will remember how my wife and my half-sister spent conspiratorial minutes by the champagne fountain, how my father looked with sincere pride at me and all I've become. And I'll try not to think of Flora and her death, but I will think of her, and I'll wonder if this day of joy balances out her days of pain or her day of death, and I will not know the answer.

A Note From the Author

First off, I'd like to thank Kevin Morgan Watson and the staff at Press 53 for bringing this book into existence. Your hard work and enthusiasm for my writing—in this book and in various Press 53 anthologies—is truly heartening. I would also like to thank David Bowen, Duff Brenna, Andrew Hudgins, Sean Karns, Thomas E. Kennedy, Kyle Minor, David R. Slavitt, and Jillian Weise for continued friendship and support in matters both personal and literary. Big thanks to Jenna Bowen for reading the novella in this collection and offering editorial suggestions (and for being generally wonderful). I would also like to thank Lee K. Abbott, Lee Martin, and Erin McGraw—my fiction teachers at Ohio State University. And last, but certainly not least, I would like to thank Raul Clement, who has read and edited every story in this collection, sometimes more than once. You are my first, last, and best reader, Raul. I thank you for all the years of friendship and for playing the Ezra to this lesser Elliott. Raul also collaborated with me on "The Long Walk Home" in this collection, which was a great pleasure, as all of our collaborations are.

OKLA ELLIOTT is currently the Illinois Distinguished Fellow at the University of Illinois, where he works in the fields of comparative literature and trauma studies. He also holds an MFA from Ohio State University. For the academic year 2008-09, he was a visiting assistant professor at Ohio Wesleyan University. His drama, non-fiction, poetry, short fiction, and translations have appeared in *Another Chicago Magazine, Indiana Review, The Literary Review, Natural Bridge, New Letters, A Public Space,* and *The Southeast Review,* among others. He is the author of three poetry chapbooks—*The Mutable Wheel; Lucid Bodies and Other Poems;* and *A Vulgar Geography*—and he co-edited (with Kyle Minor) *The Other Chekhov.*

From the Crooked Timber is his debut short story collection.

Cover artist IVANA KRUŠEC is a hobby photographer from Zagreb, Croatia, where she developed her passion for nature photography. Driven by desire to immortalize nature's beauty, she has been sharing her works for the past six years on Flickr at www.flickr.com/cvrcak.

CPSIA information can be obtained at www.ICGtesting.com
Printed in the USA
LVOW041412161111

255281LV00001B/45/P